The day that SHOULD HAVE changed THE WORLD

Barry Woodhouse

First published in Great Britain as a softback original in 2023

Design, typesetting and publishing by UK Book Publishing

www.ukbookpublishing.com

ISBN: 978-1-915338-86-0

Dedicated to the young men of
Royal Air Force Bomber Command
United States Army Air Force 8th Air Force
United States Army Air Force 15th Air Force
who gave their lives on combat missions over
Germany and occupied Europe during the
Second World War.

With our eternal gratitude.

Other titles by the author

Tring. A Pictorial History. Phillimore & Co Ltd.
ISBN 1 86077 017 7

Tring Born & Bred. Monroe Publishing.
ISBN 0 9532938 0 7

The Stabber of the Sky. UK Book Publishing.
ISBN 9781912183210

One Gunner's War. UK Book Publishing.
(In My Grandfather's Footsteps)
ISBN 978 1 912183 84 5

Contents

Prologue

The reader should first be made aware of some historical facts which will be of assistance in fully understanding the claims made within this book. I will make references to just a few of the Allied deceptions employed during World War Two although further investigation by the reader is encouraged and will reveal far more information. I also make reference to attempts on Hitler's life by members of his hierarchy.

The Allied deceptions, which are covered in more detail in this book, were given various codenames. Operation Mincemeat; a bold and extremely risky plan to convince the Germans that the planned invasion of Sicily was just a feint for another operation. Operation Fortitude; a brilliant plan in which Australian born actor Meyrick Edward Clifton James impersonated Field Marshall Montgomery completely fooling the German High Command. A third involved a small time crook who was recruited by British intelligence as a double agent, Eddie Chapman, code named Zig Zag, who successfully infiltrated German spy networks.

But we must not forget the numerous attempts made on Adolf Hitler's life; again further investigation by the reader is encouraged. I mention just two such attempts although there were many more which all failed resulting in the plotters either being executed or sent to concentration camps where they undoubtedly met their end in the cruelest of circumstances.

Possibly the best known is the 'Wolf's Lair' plot of July 1944. Again this is detailed more fully within this book. This is just one of the many failed attempts on Adolf Hitler's life. Why did some senior officers in the German armed forces desire their Fuhrer's death and rid Germany of the Third Reich and Nazism? Who were they, and what was their eventual fate?

Then we have Albert Speer, who was Reich Minister of Armaments and War Production, who claims to have attempted to assassinate Adolf Hitler with a poison gas canister placed in an external ventilator shaft at the Chancellery bunker in March 1945 in Berlin. There is some doubt as to the truth behind this claim by Speer.

The fall of Berlin to the Russian Army in May 1945 and Hitler's remains discovered at the Bunker are critical to the evidence presented in this book. Was the charred body really that of Adolf Hitler? Or was it in fact, a 'double,' which was meant to fool the world into believing that Adolf Hitler was finally dead? There is evidence to show that he did in fact escape to South America aboard one of two German submarines with other prominent Nazis, taking looted gold where he remained for the remainder of his life under the protection of other Nazis and government officials. Personally I doubt if the world will ever know the truth, although I am persuaded to believe that he did in fact evade justice by escaping to South America.

To fully understand this German deception that was perpetrated by the SS and Heinrich Himmler, it will be of assistance to the reader to have some basic knowledge of Dachau Concentration Camp that is central to this story. A brief explanation of its creation in 1933 and the reasons for its and other such concentration camps existence is explained briefly.

All of these deceptions and assassination attempts are directly linked to this amazing story that at times does appear to be beyond belief. This story has never been told before. It is the story of one of the greatest deceptions of World War Two and even of recent history. It was an incredible deception on the German side, which was so cleverly executed, that all of Hitler's closest aides and his Chief of Staff were unaware that it was taking place. The deception continued through the last days of the war and was to continue even after the German unconditional surrender to the Allied Forces in May 1945.

The operational details described in Chapter One of this book are of an actual bombing operation carried out on 4 November 1944 as described in a record of the tour of operations carried out by No. 626 Squadron from RAF Wickenby, compiled by J. MacDonald (Sergeant, Flight Engineer) with maps by D. G. Wells (Flight Sergeant, Bomb Aimer,) both members of 626 Squadron. For the purposes of this book I have written this operation as if the bombing mission by No. 626 Squadron occurred in 1941.

Squadron Leader Douglas Joss, who was a rear gunner with this squadron at RAF Wickenby, was my Commanding Officer during my RAF service. At his funeral I was privileged to be one of his pallbearers.

Apart from actual historical figures named all other names within this novel are fictional and any resemblance to any individual, living or dead, is purely coincidental.

The Allied Deceptions and Plots Against Adolf Hitler

Tricking the enemy into believing 'the unbelievable' could make all the difference between winning or loosing a campaign and even the final outcome of any war. The Allies, during World War Two, were particularly successful at achieving this.

'Operation Mincemeat' was a daring British plan to deceive the German High Command into believing that the Allies would not invade Sicily, although in reality, they fully intended to. This true story is described in every detail in Ewen Montagu's book 'The Man Who Never Was', (Lieutenant Commander Ewen Montagu was the officer in charge of the deception) and was put into operation during 1942 and 1943.

Lieutenant Commander Ewen Montagu, born 1901, was the second son of the 2nd Baron Swaythling, Louis Samuel Montagu. Educated at Westminster School, he became a machine gunner instructor in the United States of America during World War l. In World War II he served in the British Naval Intelligence Division, with the rank of Lieutenant Commander, Royal Navy Volunteer Reserve (RNVR). 'Operation Mincemeat' was the combined idea of himself and Squadron Leader Charles Cholmondely, Royal Air Force Volunteer Reserve (RAFVR). For his role in 'Operation Mincemeat', Montagu was awarded the Military Order of the British Empire.

This daring plan was to say the least, very bizarre. On the 30th of April 1943 the body of a civilian, 34-year-old Welshman Glyndwr Michael, who had recently died of natural causes was selected to be used in this plan as he had no living relations as both parents were already dead and there were no known other family members. For the plan to work the body had to be that of a man who had the appearance of hypothermia and drowning at sea.

Lieutenant Commander Ewen Montagu obtained his body, and after the false identification of a 'Major William Martin' was produced for the body, it was then dressed in an officer's uniform of the Royal Marines. (The name "Martin" was chosen because there were several other officers with the same surname and of about that rank in the Royal Marines. This was hoped to confuse any investigations by German intelligence.)

Major Martin's identity was created as being assigned to Headquarters, Combined Operations, where he would come under the control of the Admiralty. False identity papers placed on the body gave his date of birth as 1907 and he was born in Cardiff, Wales. The briefcase containing the plans for the invasion of North Africa, together with personal letters from his fiancé, Pam, and also a photograph of her. ('Pam' was actually a genuine person. Her real name was Jean Leslie, a clerk working for MI5.) Love letters from her were also included in Major Martin's wallet. These letters were written, it is believed, either by Hester Leggett or a Victoire Evelyn Bennett. The briefcase was chained to his wrist (normal security procedure) and the body was then transported in a sealed container and taken aboard a Royal Navy submarine, HMS Dasher, where after several days sailing submerged to avoid detection, the body was released into the waters at Huelva just off of the coast of Spain, where, it was hoped, the body and briefcase would eventually be washed ashore and the briefcase find its way into the hands of the German Embassy. (Although Spain was officially neutral, the Spanish Government was sympathetic to the German cause because of the German Luftwaffe's assistance during the Spanish Civil War some years earlier.) The plan worked and the German's believed that the details of the invasion were genuine, which of course, they were not.

A film of the same name was produced in the 1950's, and although following the book in most respects the film went on to include the involvement of an Irishman employed as a German agent. That part of the film is pure fiction however. A little known fact is that in the film Ewen Montagu played the role of a senior Royal Air Force officer who criticised his own character - played by actor Clifton Webb, during a briefing for the operation!

Originally Glyndwr Michael was buried under his assumed name (Major Martin,) in Huelva cemetery in Spain. After investigation however, his true identity was uncovered and his headstone now includes his real name.

Double agents, that is, spies who were employed by both the Allies and German secret services, could prove to be very useful and an excellent way to gain information and also to 'plant' false and misleading intelligence to the enemy. One risk in using these so called 'double agents' was the uncertainty in both of their individual spy masters minds as to where their loyalty actually lay, unless of course, they had no loyalty to either side and were only interested in the financial gains that both sides offered. But that apart, these 'double agents' were extremely brave people, having to be doubly sure that they could prove and maintain their loyalty and usefulness, for whatever reasons, to their masters.

One such British 'double agent' was Eddie Chapman, code name 'Zig Zag'. A professional safecracker and small time crook, he was imprisoned in the Channel Islands after being sentenced for various crimes he had committed on the English mainland. He was still imprisoned there at the time of the German invasion of these islands. After making himself known to the German Commandant of the prison and offering his services to the Third Reich he was eventually recruited by the Germans as a spy and saboteur. The Germans realized that his ability to think quickly if compromised or caught, and his prison record, including safe breaking, would be a tremendous asset in his role as a German spy. Known as Fritz or Fritzchen, he became regarded as a prime agent, even being awarded the Iron Cross for his service to the Third Reich.

It was on a mission to England that he made contact with the British police. Eventually the British Secret Service was contacted and after some time attempting to prove that his loyalties were to England, was recruited as a 'double agent'. His German mission was to destroy the aircraft manufacturing facility at de Havilland's plant in Hatfield, a plan that went ahead although the resulting explosions and damage was faked to convince his German masters that he had carried out his mission with great success.

Chapman even offered at one point to assassinate Adolf Hitler and even devised a plan to carry this out. His German master, von Groning, an Abwehr officer he knew only as "Dr. Graumann", had promised Chapman that he would arrange a meeting with Hitler; it was at this meeting that Chapman would carry out his plan. The British, who were not convinced that Chapman was capable of carrying out his wild idea, vetoed it of course. Readers can discover more about Eddie Chapman in a book entitled 'Agent Zig Zag' by Ben Macintyre.

Yet another plan to deceive the Germans, was the incredible idea to trick them about the timing and place of the invasion of Europe on D-Day in 1944 - 'Operation Fortitude'. The British XX Committee, which came to be known both as the 'Twenty Committee' and 'Double-cross', gradually expanded its activities and eventually concluded that it had effectively taken control of the Abwehr's (German Army) entire spy network in Britain. It was with skillful handling and the careful cross-referencing of information from agents with intercepted German wireless communications that allowed MI5 an unprecedented insight into the enemy's intentions, and the development of a sophisticated conduit for conveying deception to the enemy.

Thirteen German agents were executed in Britain during the war, but more than three times that number had been 'turned' and actively co-operated with their MI5 handlers. Better to work for the British Intelligence Service than face execution by hanging or firing squad.

By 1944 MI5 was sufficiently confident of its double agents that they could be entrusted with 'Operation Fortitude', the principal deception campaign intended to persuade the Germans that the widely expected Allied invasion of France would occur in the Pas-de-Calais. A secondary objective was to convey the impression that the landings in Normandy were merely a diversionary feint that could be safely ignored.

'Fortitude' became a textbook example of how strategic deception should be conducted. Captured German documents examined after the war demonstrated that the enemy was duped not just about the date and place of the main Allied offensive, but had even accepted that an entirely fictional army, the First United States Army Group, had assembled in south-east England in anticipation of crossing the English Channel from Dover. To make this 'ghost' army appear even more genuine it was commanded by the very well known American General, 'Old Blood and Guts' George Patton, who, at the time, was in disgrace for his violent outburst towards an American soldier in hospital suffering from combat fatigue, better known as 'shell shock'.

British actor Meyrick Edward Clifton James, born in Perth, Australia in 1898, serving in the British Army Pay Corps, played a vital and major part. Several months before the long planned D-Day invasion landings in 1944, Lieutenant Colonel, J.V.B. Jervis-Reid, noticed his remarkable resemblance to Montgomery. (Clifton James had made an appearance in an amateur stage show actually playing Montgomery.) MI5 decided to use his uncanny resemblance in a proposed operation linked with the invasion of Europe. He was contacted by Lieutenant-Colonel David Niven, (another British actor) at the time working for the Army's film unit, and was asked to come to London with the cover story of making a propaganda film. Clifton James impression of Montgomery was so convincing that he was approached with the idea to 'replace' Montgomery to enable the 'genuine' Montgomery to press ahead with planning the D-Day landings without the German's being aware. His successful portrayal of Field Marshal Montgomery tricked the Germans into believing that the Allies would attack from elsewhere on the European mainland. The success of this resulted in the German military moving men and equipment to Calais where they firmly believed the Allies would land. This would mean that thousands of Allied lives would be saved on the invasion beaches and the advance inland.

This particular D-Day deception used by the Allies to feed false information and mislead the German High Command was brilliant, and can be compared to the story in this book. The remarkable differences however, are that the German plan continued for many years - even after hostilities ceased in 1945, and more remarkably it was conceived by factions within the German High Command - albeit after being forced upon them!

The 'Wolf's Lair' July Plot

On July 20th 1944 an attempt to assassinate Hitler took place at the 'Wolf's Lair' - Wolfsschanze - Hitler's headquarters in the pine forests of Rastenburg in Eastern Prussia. It was here that a group of conspirators led by Lieutenant Colonel Claus von Stauffenberg, who was on the General Staff of the Reserve Army in Berlin, attempted to kill Adolf Hitler.

Claus Philipp Maria Graf Schenk von Stauffenberg was born on 15th of November 1907, and was a German army officer and Catholic aristocrat. He was one of the leading members of the failed 'Wolf's Lair' plot to kill Adolf Hitler and remove the Nazi Party from power in World War II Germany. Along with Henning von Tresckow and Hans Oster, he was one of the central figures of the German Resistance movement within the Wehrmacht (German Army). He served with distinction during the North African campaign. However when American aircraft strafed his motor vehicle he was severely wounded, losing an eye and arm. After many months in hospital recovering from his wounds he was transferred to Berlin and it was while in Berlin that Lieutenant Colonel Claus von Stauffenberg began to make contact with other German leaders involved in an anti-Hitler movement that was sworn to eliminating Adolf Hitler and sue for a honourable peace with the Allies. These conspirators were anti-Nazis and realised that Germany had no chance of winning the war.

The meeting on this fateful day, 20th July, was held in the conference hut and not the command bunker. The plotters would have preferred the concrete command bunker to attempt to assassinate Hitler, as the effects of the blast would be greater than in the weaker structure of the wooden conference hut which would disperse the blast effect and lessen the chance of killing Hitler and hopefully, other high ranking German officers. Claus von Stauffenberg placed within a few feet of Hitler, a briefcase, holding the bomb. History records that Adolf Hitler, although wounded, survived this assassination attempt.

The conspirators were quickly arrested by General Friedrich Fromm, Commander-in-Chief of the Replacement Army, (also a suspected conspirator), who held an impromptu court martial and condemned the ringleaders of the conspiracy to death. Lieutenant Colonel Claus von Stauffenberg, along with fellow officers General Olbricht, Lieutenant von Haeften and Oberst Albrecht Mertz von Quirnheim, were later shot that same night by firing squad, hastily drawn together by Fromm, in the courtyard of the War Ministry. As von Stauffenberg's time of execution came he spoke his last words - "Es lebe unser heiliges Deutschland!" ("Long live our sacred Germany!"). Believed to be troubled by his actions, General Fromm gave the executed officers a Military burial, their army campaign medals and other awards still intact on their uniforms. The following day von Stauffenberg's body was exhumed and he was stripped of his medals and burned.

As for the other conspirators; Major General Hermann Karl Robert von Tresckow, Generals Otto von Stulpnagel, Beck, and Hoeppner, Field Marshals' von Witzleben, von Kluge and Admiral Canaris; they were arrested, tortured and finally executed by being hung from hooks by piano wire. Some conspirators took their own lives when news of the failed attempt was broadcast on German radio. A number of prominent civilians who were involved in the bomb plot also received the same fate by the SS after so called 'trials'.

This was not the only attempt on Hitler's life. Many assassination attempts were planned, not only by German anti Nazis, but also by the British Special Operations Executive (SOE). But despite all of these elaborate schemes only one was to succeed and even the SOE was unaware that Hitler had finally been eliminated!

Today in a united Germany, Claus von Stauffenberg is remembered as a national hero. He is a revered symbol of German resistance to the Nazi regime. The courtyard where Claus von Stauffenberg and his fellow officers were shot is now a National site of remembrance. Displayed is a plaque commemorating the events of July 1944. A bronze figure of a man, his hands bound symbolically, also stands there.

Operation Foxley and the SOE

Operation Foxley was a plot conceived by the British Special Operations Executive (SOE). If carried out it could have shortened the war saving possibly millions of lives. Approved by many members of the British Government including Winston Churchill, it was rejected on the grounds that Adolf Hitler was actually helping the Allied cause by some of the decisions he was making in conducting the war. Initially the plan called for an attack on Hitler's private train the 'Amerika' by placing a bomb on board or poisoning the train's water supply. These ideas were rejected as it needed an inside agent to carry out either plan.

However after the Normandy landings in France on 6 June 1944 one of Hitler's personal guards was captured and interrogated by members of the SOE. They discovered that he had actually served Hitler at his mountain retreat in Bavaria – the Berghof. The SOE learnt that whenever Hitler was in residence the swastika flag was flown which could be seen from a café in the nearby town of Berchtesgaden below the Berghof. They also learnt of Hitler's daily routine particularly at what times he took his daily walks, usually alone.

Allied air reconnaissance photographs showed clearly the path that Hitler would take, one section which took Hitler outside of the estate just several hundred yards from a wooded area, where is was suggested a sniper could lay in wait and at the first opportunity shoot Hitler. A bold plan, but who could carry out this scheme? It was decided that a fluent German speaking Polish national was best suited. He had to be a first rate marksman and both physically fit and mentally agile. This was not to be a suicide mission; these requirements would give the assassin the best opportunity to escape. The SOE eventually decided upon two agents, a German speaking Pole and a British sniper. Both would be parachuted into the area dressed as German soldiers.

With everything prepared and the operation ready to proceed in November 1944 it was suggested by Lieutenant Colonel Ronald Thornley who was deputy head of SOE's

German Directorate, that killing Hitler was really not a very good idea. Hitler was running the war as he saw fit ignoring his General Staff and as such was making demands on the German armed forces that were beyond their capability to carry out successfully. To kill him might just mean that his army Generals could have run a successful strategy and at least been able to barter for good surrender terms, or if the war was lost then the German population could claim that if Hitler had lived the war might have been won. And so the operation was shelved and Adolf Hitler was allowed to live as the SOE believed that he would in effect lose the war for Germany.

Albert Speer

Albert Speer, as Reich Minister of Armaments and War Production, claimed during the Nuremberg War Trials that he turned against Hitler in the latter stages of the Second World War and planned to assassinate him by pumping poison gas through a ventilation shaft into the Fuhrer Bunker in Berlin. (At the time of writing there is doubt by many historians as to whether this is true. It is believed that Speer was attempting to show to the court that he was not a Nazi and knew nothing of the many deaths of slave workers who were used to produce arms for the Nazi war machine.)

He was found guilty of war crimes and crimes against humanity, principally for the use of slave labor and forced labour of which he denied any knowledge of. He also claimed that he was not aware of Nazi extermination camps or of the Holocaust. This probably saved him from hanging. He was sentenced to 20 years imprisonment on October 1st 1946. Having served his full term he was released in 1966.

Dachau Concentration Camp

MARCH 1933 - MAY 1945

In March of 1933, Heinrich Himmler decided to build a new concentration camp run by his infamous SS. SS or Schutzstaffel translated literally it means 'Protective Squad'. Originally acting as bodyguards for leading members of the Nazi party and regarded by Nazis as an elite unit often referred to as the Party's "praetorian guard". All SS personnel were selected on the principles of racial purity and unconditional loyalty to their Führer, Adolf Hitler, and the Nazi Party. The military branch of the SS, the Waffen SS, evolved into a second German army in addition to the regular German army, the Wehrmacht. A fanatical fighting force, they were feared by even the Wehrmacht.

The first of many such camps was Dachau, opened during March 1933 and located approximately ten to twelve miles (16 to 18 kilometers) north of Munich on the Amper River in the grounds of a former munitions factory. To organise this new camp, Himmler selected a fanatical SS member, Theodor Eicke. Eicke was so successful in this project that he earned the nickname 'Father of Concentration Camps'.

'Arbiet Macht Frei' - or 'Work Sets You Free', greeted all new prisoners to Dachau. It was placed above the gates as a 'welcome' to new prisoners. Most of these first inmates were classified as political prisoners, but were mostly unfortunate enough to have had problems with the German police or had been 'denounced' by people who had a reason to dislike them and wanted to exact revenge on them.

Originally planned to hold no more than 5,000 prisoners, this number was increased as more 'undesirables', namely gypsies, Jews, anti Nazis, and any German citizen who made themselves unpopular with the Nazi party, were imprisoned here. A total of 206,000 prisoners were registered in Dachau in the 12 years it existed. Over 32,000 prisoners were registered as dying at the camp during this same period but many deaths were never recorded so the final total can only be estimated. It will never be known how many died during the final 'death march' when 7,000 prisoners were forced to move before the camp could be liberated by the rapidly advancing American forces.

On 26 April 1945 camp prisoner Karl Riemer escaped from Dachau to get help from approaching American troops. An agreement to surrender the camp, negotiated by the International Red Cross, was agreed on the 28th and the camp was surrendered to American forces. That night a secret committee was set up in the camp before its liberation - The Comite International de Dachau's took over the control of the camp. Its aim was to prevent any last minute mass extermination by the SS. Members of the SS who were captured by the American forces were then held in the camp itself until they could be tried for War Crimes. Many of these guards were attempting to evade capture by posing as inmates, but their well-fed appearance stood out amongst the starving inmates and they were arrested. Prisoners identified many of these guards as being guilty of the most brutal atrocities carried out at the camp.

Units of 3rd Battalion, 157th Infantry Regiment, 45th Infantry Division, commanded by Lieutenant Colonel Felix L. Sparks, were ordered to secure the camp, his troops entered by climbing over a sidewall. Formal surrender of the camp took place on April 29 and was accepted by Brigadier General Henning Linden from German Lieutenant Heinrich

Wicker at the entrance between the main camp and the compound for the SS garrison. More than 30,000 Jewish and political prisoners were freed. These survivors accounted for over 30 different nationalities held within the camp.

The Germans were fanatical about keeping records, and Dachau Concentration Camp was no exception. These records were examined in great detail by a special Allied detachment gathering information for use after the war in the War Crimes trials to prosecute members of the SS for not only War Crimes but also for Crimes against Humanity.

The Fall of Berlin

APRIL 15TH - MAY 2ND 1945

The Battle for Berlin ended on the 2nd of May 1945. Soviet troops claimed that the silence that followed the fall of Berlin 'was deafening'. A little over 3 years since Hitler's armed forces had invaded the Soviet Union with the commencement of 'Operation Barbarossa', the 'Thousand Year Reich' had collapsed and Hitler was dead.

Stalin had always intended to take Berlin before his Western Allies. To achieve this aim the lives of some 70,000 Russian soldiers were lost. The total cost in lives on both sides will probably never be known, but it was many tens, if not hundreds, of thousands..

For two years before the fall of Berlin, Bomber Command of the Royal Air Force together with the USAAF 8th and 15th Air Forces had bombed Berlin day and night. That, together with the millions of artillery shells fired into the city in the final weeks of the war by the Russian

Army had left Berlin in total ruins. It is estimated that some 250,000 German civilians died in the final weeks before Berlin eventually fell and Germany surrendered.

The Soviet Union deployed 2,500,000 troops, 6,000 tanks and more than 40,000 artillery pieces in the Battle for Berlin. In comparison the German forces consisted of just 300,000 Wehrmacht troops, the remains of the once mighty German army, together with old men and Hitler Youth conscripted into the army in the defence of Berlin.

Why was Stalin so determined to take Berlin before his Allies? Consider these facts. Since the invasion of the Soviet Union (Operation Barbarossa) by Germany, the Soviet Union had lost in excess of 23,000,000 soldiers and civilians; whole villages had been burnt to the ground, the occupants tortured and murdered. Children were shot, women raped and vast areas of Russia had been laid to waste. Stalin, and the Soviet soldiers, were seeking retribution and justice.

The Russian Army, under the commands of Marshal Zhukov (Army Group Centre) and Marshal Konev (Army Group South), were deliberately 'pitted' against each other by Stalin in his race for Berlin. Each of his two Marshals were intent on taking Berlin before the other. The offensive commenced on 15th April 1945. It took Zukhov three days of heavy fighting to break through into Berlin. German resistance was fierce, with some 30,000 Soviet soldiers killed and over 10,000 German casualties.

On or about the 22nd April, inside Hitler's bunker, Hitler decided to stand and fight for Berlin, with Hitler personally controlling the defence of his capital city. Hitler ordered General Wenck's 70,000 troops of the 12th Army to unite with General Busse's 9th Army to launch a counter attack against the Soviet Army.

Marshal Konev's army intercepted and surrounded these forces at Halbe, and a fierce battle ensued in the woodland there. More than 50,000 German soldiers and civilians were slaughtered in these woods. This could be claimed to be the last stand by German SS and Wermacht forces in the defence of Berlin.

It was Marshal Zhukov who was to be the first to enter Berlin, capital of the Third Reich. The Reich that was to last for 'a thousand years' would soon be over. Fierce fighting by 90,000 German defenders, the last defiant remnants of the once mighty German Army and SS units, together with squads of the Hitler Youth and old men armed with panzerfaust (anti-tank rocket launcher's) had cost the lives of countless thousands of soldiers and civilians alike.

These 90,000 poorly equipped combatants faced more than 1,000,000 battle hardened Soviet troops and thousands of T34 tanks and artillery pieces. By the 2nd of May, the Reichstag (the old German Parliament) had fallen. While thousands were dying in the streets and ruined buildings of what was left of the German capital, under the garden at the Reich Chancellery, Hitler, together with Josef Goebbels, Martin Bormann and other Nazi leaders, were gathered together in the bunker. A remarkable event had just taken place; Hitler had at long last married Eva Braun, on the stroke of midnight.

Hitler wore the same style of tunic that he wore after he went to war with the invasion of Poland; Eva Braun was wearing a long silk black dress for the ceremony. The 'approved' Nazi wedding ceremony consisted of the wedding official - an official from the Propaganda Ministry - asking the Fuhrer and Eva Braun to confirm that they were both of pure Aryan descent and were free from any hereditary diseases.

The actual ceremony took no longer than five minutes. The register was duly signed and witnessed by Josef Goebbels and Martin Bormann. Eva Braun almost signed the register in her maiden name, but stopped, and crossing through the 'B' correctly signed as 'Eva Hitler nee Braun'.

The couple then went through to the conference room in the bunker to be greeted by Generals and various secretaries who congratulated them both. Hitler, apparently, was so nervous that he was visibly shaking. (Hitler at this time was being administered vast amounts of drugs by his personal physician Theodor Gilbert Morell. He was known in Germany for being unconventional in his medical treatments. Although he was licensed as a general practitioner he was regarded as a 'quack' after he was captured and questioned by the Allies. It is now believed by many historians that his medical treatment prescribed to Hitler contributed to his ill health.) Retiring to a sitting room, they had a champagne wedding breakfast. Eva Braun now insisted on being called Frau Hitler.

Whilst this was taking place, just a few hundred yards away outside the bunker, the few remaining defenders of Berlin, elder civilians recruited to fight alongside the SS and Hitler Youth, were suffering from the dust and smoke of war, thirst and hunger, and dying in a futile defence of Berlin. None obviously had any knowledge as to the events inside the bunker or what was about to happen.

News had come through to Hitler that Mussolini had been executed and had been strung up with his mistress, Clara Petacci. When did Hitler finally accept that the war was lost? That is not known for certain, but on hearing this news Hitler became obsessed that his body would be taken to Moscow to be put on display. He had grave doubts that cyanide capsules would work. (He believed that he would only be drugged to render him unconscious, so that he could be taken against his will to Allied forces attacking from the west). So it was arranged that his beloved German Shepherd bitch 'Blondi' should be taken up to the gardens above the bunker and be poisoned to see if the cyanide would work. Her puppies were also killed in the same manner.

Inside the bunker events were taking place which would sicken the civilised world. The Goebbels children were ruthlessly murdered by their own parents, and were found laying along side each other, as if asleep, by Soviet troops. Did these children really deserve this end? Hadn't there been enough suffering and murder committed by the Nazi party? But the suicides were not yet over.

Hitler's valet, Heinz Linge, entered Hitler's room and found Hitler slumped over his desk. He had committed suicide by shooting himself in the right temple with a .765 pistol. Hitler's body was wrapped in a Werhmact blanket by, it is believed, Goebbels, Borman and Hitler Youth leader, Artur Axmann. The corpse was taken out into the corridor and then up the stairs into the Reich Chancellery garden. Eva Braun's body was found 'curled up' on a couch near Hitler's body - she had taken cyanide - and was laid next to Hitler's body. Both bodies were then drenched in petrol and set alight. This proved to be difficult at first, as there was a stiff breeze blowing, which continually blew the matches out. A rolled up sheet of paper was produced which was lit, and then thrown onto the two corpses, which finally caught fire.

Berlin finally surrendered to Marshal Zhukov on the 2nd of May. The battle had cost over 70,000 Russian casualties with many Soviet units being decimated and all but wiped out in their haste to take Berlin. The final death toll on the German defenders side is not known but must have been many tens of thousands.

Hitler's remains were discovered by Russian soldiers and removed to Moscow under the tightest of security and secrecy where they were hidden away for many years until the 'Cold War' finally came to an end. Even to this day, more than 75 years after the end of the war, there still remains doubt as to whether the bodies found by the Soviets were in fact those of Hitler and Eva Braun. The bodies were both burnt beyond recognition and although extensive scientific tests were carried out on the remains in the 1980's their identity have never been conclusively established. One question has always remained and never really answered - "Were they in fact the remains of Adolf Hitler and Eva Braun?"

The story you are about to read is based on historical fact. It explains why many of the military decisions made by Adolf Hitler were to bring doom to the German people and end the 'Thousand Year' Third Reich.

But you, the reader, must arrive at your own conclusion. Did Adolf Hitler really commit suicide, or was it a very elaborate hoax? Newspaper reports from April 1945 first brought to the attention of the Allies that a double did in fact exist. Included in the end pages of this book are photographs of the newspaper article and an even more remarkable photograph of Hitler's double that was apparently discovered shot in the grounds above the bunker. There appears to be no visible signs of the body being burnt.

This and possibly other photographs of the corpse were suppressed by the Allied powers for fears that Nazi party members who had either managed to escape overseas or had vanished amongst the ruins of Germany and Berlin, and indeed the German Nation, would continue to support their Fuhrer.

The day that SHOULD HAVE changed THE WORLD

Chapter 1

Our Story Begins

4 NOVEMBER 1941

At some time shortly after midnight Avro Lancaster bombers from 626 Squadron based at RAF Wickenby in Lincolnshire were returning home to their base after delivering their deadly cargo of high explosives to their target into the heart of the Third Reich.

Many of the returning bombers were spread out across the night sky across Germany and occupied Europe. Occasionally our Lancaster - 'G' George - would hit the slip stream of another aircraft somewhere in the darkness ahead of us forcing our pilot to take violent evasive action to avoid a mid air collision, for that to happen after enduring flak and German night fighters would be just too much bad luck! Brought down over enemy territory by one of our own bombers! Just another three hours would see us approaching our base for a safe landing after what had turned out to be a fairly easy operation - too easy.

The previous day was a particularly chilly one. The fluttering of lightly falling early snow was being brushed along the surface of the airfield by a blustery wind, much like a sand storm, before finally settling into small drifts against the sides of various buildings on the airfield.

At the operation briefing in the afternoon before the night's operation, the squadrons were given all the information that each bomber crew would need to make this mission as successful and as safe as possible. Navigators took note of the route to take and their aircraft's bombing time over the target, this was to avoid mid-air collisions as bombers would be over the target for possibly several hours in a bombing stream several miles long and staggered at various heights. Over 700 bombers mainly made up of Avro Lancasters, Halifaxes, and with a few now almost retired from service, ancient Short Stirlings, would be taking part tonight, from half a dozen bases scattered throughout the county of Lincolnshire in the eastern region of England. Lincolnshire was an ideal bomber county being flat with few if any hills to threaten returning bombers that may have suffered damage caused by flak or night fighters and were flying at a low altitude returning to base.

Timing over the target was crucial. If you arrived too early you ran the risk of other bombers flying in a higher 'stream' than you dropping their bomb load on top of your bomber with deadly results, but arrive too late and the anti aircraft gunners and searchlight crews thousands of feet on the ground below would be searching for late arrivals and be on full alert ready to shoot you out of the sky.

A total force of 336 Lancasters, 384 Halifaxes and 29 Mosquitos were to take part in tonight's operation. 32 of the Lancaster force would be from Wickenby of which 18 would be from 626 Squadron. Fighter cover would be comprised of seven squadrons of Mustangs and 16 squadrons of Spitfires. The target was to be the industrial centre of the Rhur with the Nordstern Synthetic Oil Plant at Gelsenkirchen being the primary target for 34 of the Lancasters including those from 626 Squadron. Other targets were allocated to other groups.

Oboe equipped Mosquitos would mark the aiming point with red TIs (Target Indicators) throughout the attack. Other PFF (Path Finder Force) aircraft would back this up with mixed indicators of red and green TIs. Three Master Bomber Lancaster aircraft would also be taking part in directing the bomber crews where to place their bomb load. Take off from Wickenby commenced at 14.59 hours. The bomb load for the Lancasters of 626 Squadron would be a total of 12,280lbs for each aircraft, comprising of 1 x 4,000 HE (high explosive) bomb and 2,070 x 4lb incendiaries.

At the briefing Flying Officer Cato our weather forecaster - better known as the 'met man' - predicted that en-route there would be 5/10ths cloud with tops at 10,000 feet over England, increasing over the North Sea to give 10/10ths cloud at the Dutch coast. The cloud was predicted to gradually break up over the Ruhr Valley with large gaps in the cloud once over the target so the crews should be able to identify the target visually, but how many times had the crews been told that only to find that the target was totally obscured and they had to press on to a secondary target that, hopefully, was fairly free of cloud! If they couldn't drop their bomb load then they would have to bring them back, and when over the North Sea jettison them in a designated safe area where there would be no risk to shipping. These areas - there was another dropping area in the English Channel - were known to all Allied ships and as such they would steer clear to avoid being accidentally bombed.

The Navigating Officer was next. The route would take the bomber formation south of Amsterdam as it crossed the Dutch coast, it would then turn on a more southerly course aiming for the German city of Bochum situated between Essen and Dortmund. Once the targets had been attacked the bomber stream would continue for some miles before turning south and then head south west before finally turning north west to return to their bases in England passing close to Brussels and Courtai.

Briefing over all that was left to do now was to check that their individual Lancaster was 'signed off' as being airworthy. 'Signing' off an aircraft, any type of aircraft from the fastest fighter to the slowest bomber and all those in between, was one of those military bits of paper that simply put, meant that the pilot was taking the aircraft as being 'airworthy and fit for purpose'. Without his signature on the form, that aircraft would not be flying on this or any other raid.

The air gunners marched off to the armoury to collect their .303 machine guns, and together with the assistance of squadron armourers, remount them in the various turret places. Belts of ammunition would be checked and fed into the machine gun breeches ready for test firing once the Lancaster was on its way to the target for tonight. There were three gun positions on a Lancaster; front turret with two machine-guns; mid-upper with two, and the rear turret with four. The coldest and most isolated place on a Lancaster was this rear turret. Once enclosed in the tiniest of spaces with the door firmly closed the only communication gunner had was via the intercom system. Unlike the rest of the crew who were within eye contact with each other he was completely isolated and on his own.

Many experienced rear gunners better known as Tail End Charlies, actually cut out the Perspex windshield in front of the turret to prevent any refracting light from enemy searchlights blinding them interfering with their night vision. Ground crews would polish this Perspex panel and over time would leave minute scratches on its surface thus diffusing the light. Very similar to driving a car at night with a smeared windscreen, any approaching car headlights will have the same effect making driving very difficult. Dead flies on the screen could even give the appearance of enemy night fighters approaching against the night sky. The purpose of cutting away the screen was to eliminate these problems, but it added another. The gunner by being open to the elements was subjected to much more inclement weather, rain and snow and freezing cold at altitude. At the time he was the only member of the crew who was issued with an electrically heated suit. A great help in keeping the cold at bay - when it worked!

A typical mixed bomb load would amount to a maximum weight of 14,000 lbs (6,350 kg). This would vary depending on the target. A long flight would mean the bomb load would be sacrificed to permit more fuel to be carried; a shorter flight and so less petrol was required, so more bombs could be carried. All of the bombers on tonight's raid carried a mixture of bombs. Ranging from 250lb bombs up to 1000lb HE bombs. Racks of incendiaries would also be dropped after the HE bombs. Their sole purpose was to set fire to the damaged industrial buildings and rubble already blasted by the HE bombs and so to inflict the maximum damage plus overwhelm the enemy fire fighters in their efforts to control and douse the flames to prevent them from spreading.

From the information given at the briefing the navigator would be busy accurately plotting the planned course onto his air charts, double-checking that his navigation equipment was in order and in 'front line' condition. It was his sole responsibility to get the bomber and its deadly load to the target at the correct time and then navigate the bomber back across enemy territory to its home base. Once over the target the bomb aimer would take over giving the pilot minor course corrections to get his cross hairs on the bomb sight over the target. With a call of "bombs away" control would be handed back to the pilot - or 'skipper' - and a course set to get back to base. The bomb aimer was a second role for the front turret gunner who would leave his gun position and move just forward and underneath to the bomb aimer's position.

Once all the aircraft checks were satisfactory carried out the crew would sometimes meet up just to 'go over things again' or return to their billets and rooms to try and snatch a few hours sleep before take off. Some crews, not being able to sleep, would play cards or write what they hoped would not be their last letter to their wife, mother and father or girl friend. Any outside communication at this stage was strictly forbidden. The letters were usually left on their bedside table to be found by their batman if they were officers, or another squadron crew member if they were NCOs (non commissioned officers) and posted should they fail to return from the mission.

The crew of 'G' George was a mixed bunch. Other crews in the squadron were not always British but were from overseas - Australians, New Zealanders, Canadians and other Allied nations. These crews tended to 'stick together' when the whole crew comprised solely of Australians, New Zealanders or Canadians. 'G' George's crew was a bit of a 'mish-mash' of all these individual nations.

Crewing up, or getting a crew together, was left to the airmen themselves to arrange and sort out. Perhaps meeting in the Station mess, or down at the local pub, it didn't really matter where, these young men would gather together for a chat and a few beers, and if they 'took' to one another would soon form a crew. If they were short of any particular member then the hunt would be on to 'nab' the missing crewman before another crew spotted him and enlisted him into their crew. Many crews were based on friendship and whether or not they 'got along' together. Sometimes this didn't always work out and the 'offending' member would look for another crew to join up with. The crew of 'G' George had been together now for some time. Tonight's mission would be their 19th, a very respectable number of operations considering the loss rate in Bomber Command at this early stage of the war.

Bomber Command started their offensive operations against Germany during day-light hours flying the American B17 Flying Fortress, but the losses were so unsustainably high that they ceased day time operations and night flying became the norm in an effort to reduce the number of mounting casualties. But a night operation has its problem as well. How to find a target at night, several hundred miles from your base? Dead reckoning and a lot of luck was the immediate answer until navigational aids such as 'Gee' and 'Oboe' came into operation.

The Lancaster's pilot, Flight Sergeant Andrew Harper, was British through and through, being born and bred in Lincolnshire. Just 21 years of age, he was married, with a young son. He joined the Royal Air Force as soon as war was declared. As an instrument maker by trade, the RAF at first offered him a job within that trade, repairing and maintaining their vast range of instruments used on all types of aircraft. But being a volunteer he pushed himself forward for aircrew, he wanted to fly, to really 'do his bit', and after passing various intelligence examinations and a full health check, was accepted for aircrew training and sent to Canada under the British Commonwealth Air Training Plan. That was almost two years ago, and is, as the old saying goes, 'all history'. It was not unusual for the pilot of any RAF aircraft to be a non commissioned officer. Regardless of his other crewmembers' ranks, it was he, and he alone, who was in command of his Lancaster. Even if he flew with a commissioned officer amongst his crew, and there were two in this crew, both Flying Officers, he was in full command of his aircraft and they had to take orders from him whilst flying - no exceptions!

There are six other crew members in our Lancaster; navigator, flight engineer, wireless operator, front turret gunner/bomb aimer, mid upper air gunner and tail gunner, better known as 'Tail End Charlie', or TEC for short.

Flight Sergeant Harper's navigator was a young Canadian, Flying Officer Arthur Baker, RCAF (Royal Canadian Air Force) from Alberta, he was just 20 years old and until now had never travelled more than a few miles outside of his home town. Leaving his nineteen-year-old fiancé in Alberta he paid his own passage across the Atlantic by steamer to England to answer his Mother countries call for volunteers as soon as war was declared. He could have easily have joined the RCAF, but being an impatient young man, decided that that would take just too long. As the navigator it was his responsibility to get the Lancaster to its target and back again, plotting the route according to the briefing orders and making allowances for wind conditions along the way. If he got it all wrong the chances are that 'G' George would not find its target or that they would find themselves in a very well defended area of the Ruhr Valley and suffer the consequences!

The flight engineer as the title implies, looks after the very life of the Lancaster - the engines. Petrol consumption must be monitored, swapping from one petrol tank to another to keep the bomber balanced and in trim as it flew; oil pressures and engine temperatures; adjusting the four engine's petrol to air mixture to ensure the best possible mix for the altitude they were to fly at. In fact he has more instruments to watch and care for than his pilot! He was the only New Zealander on board, and he regarded it as a high privilege for the rest of the crew to serve with him! Many aircrew members had a nickname and his was 'Biggles' after Captain W. E. Johns flying hero from his novels of World War l Royal Flying Corp escapades. Nobody was exactly sure why he was dubbed Biggles. Officially he was Flying Officer Sydney James McCarthy and just 22 years of age and from the tiny community of Aka Aka on the Aka Aka Stream, a tributary of the *Waikato River*, located about five miles southeast of *Waiuku*.

Next was the wireless operator. Flight Sergeant William (Bill) Walter Edney aged 24, an Australian. Bill didn't have to make a long trip from Australia to enlist. He was studying at Oxford University, and being a keen member of the University Air Squadron it took little persuasion for him to join up the day after war was declared. It was rumoured that he was too intoxicated to join up on the day! Bill was a confirmed bachelor, or was until he met the girl of his dreams in The Mitre, a local hostelry in Oxford catering mainly for students. It must have been love at first sight for both of them, for they were engaged within three weeks, their dream of a long life together being put into a slumber until he came back after the war was over when marriage and children would be their priority. Every body believed that the war really would be over by Christmas.

These four crewmembers were relatively fortunate as to their crew locations inside the Lancaster. They could all feel the benefit of a hot air heating system (diverted from the inboard starboard engine) to help keep them fairly warm when flying in the bitterly cold and rarefied air at 20,000+ feet.

The remaining three crewmembers are Sergeant Albert Grey, another Australian, aged 26 and the oldest member of the crew, affectionately known as 'Pop'. Leaving Australia some time after war was declared, he left his wife and two children in Melbourne safe in the knowledge that his mother and father would be there with them if the need ever arose. Both of his wife's parents were killed in a traffic accident and she was the only child.

His role was to plant the Lancaster's deadly load where it would do the most damage and destruction. He was the front turret gunner/bomb aimer, giving the pilot instructions via the intercom when the bomber was on its final bomb run over the target until the bombs were released and control relinquished to the pilot to turn the bomber around and head back to its base in Lincolnshire. During the outward and homeward bound flight he would take charge of the .303 twin machine guns in the front turret.

The other two air gunners; Sergeant Fred Woodhouse, affectionately known as 'Woody', who manned the mid upper position, and Pilot Officer Douglas Watson, affectionately known as 'Tiny', who was assigned as 'Tail

End Charlie', the rear gunner.

'Woody' Woodhouse and 'Tiny' Watson were both English. 'Woody', originally from the small market town of Tring in Hertfordshire, now hailed from the village of Walsoken on the Norfolk and Cambridgeshire borders, moving there as a teenager with his parents. 'Tiny' Watson was a country boy as well, born just eight miles from Tring in Weston Turville a village just a few miles from the Buckinghamshire County Town of Aylesbury. They were both roughly the same age joining the RAF within a few weeks of each other. By coincidence they were both posted to RAF Wickenby joining the same Lancaster squadron. A small world indeed!

They are responsible for the defence of the aircraft against attacks by German night fighters. 'Tiny' possibly had the most vulnerable position as rear gunner. It would be him who the German night fighters would attempt to put out of action first; kill the tail gunner and the bomber is all but defenceless from rear attacks, the favoured attacking option for the German night fighter. At six feet tall he was probably the tallest rear gunner in Bomber Command. The rest of the crew were always amazed how he could get his tall, but lean, frame into the turret without getting stuck. Silently they prayed that he would never have to bail out in an emergency, because they had serious doubts as to whether he would be able to.

'Tiny' would cause some merriment amongst his fellow air gunners and ground crew as he practised bailing out from his rear turret while on the ground. He would climb up into 'G' George, settle into his TEC position, and then rotate the turret until the access door was exposed to the outside. Having disconnected himself from all internal connections

- communications, suit electrical heater connector plug and oxygen, he would literally roll out backwards onto a couple of mattresses he had previously placed on the ground to break his fall. His explanation being that he wanted to know in advance of a "bail out" command from the pilot that he would, in fact, be capable of doing just that - bail out! Some of the other 'Tail End Charlie's' thought this was a splendid idea. For several days afterwards rear turret gunners were falling out of the turrets all over the base, much to the amusement of 'Tiny' - the laughter was on the other side now!

'Woody' Woodhouse's position was only slightly better. He sat near to Bill Edney, the wireless operator. Perched above Bill in the blister of the mid upper gun turret, his feet dangling just a few inches from Bill's head. 'Woody's' 'seat' comprised of a fairly wide strip of canvas webbing that could be clipped and unclipped to the fuselage of the Lancaster. This was his seat for the duration of the trip.

Take off time soon came, too soon for many. A quick ride on one of the Transport Sections trucks, if you were lucky enough to scrounge a lift, otherwise it could mean a long walk carrying your heavy and cumbersome parachute out to your aircraft, already standing there silently at dispersal, just waiting for its human crew to bring it to life, to do the job for which it was solely designed to do - bomb the enemy and destroy his factories and thus the means for him to carry on the war. Such was the thinking of Bomber Command, to destroy his capability to wage war and to totally demoralise the population into not wanting the war to continue.

With the crew aboard and in their assigned positions Andrew Harper, the pilot, would carry out a radio check with them to ensure that radio communications were working and that they were all at their posts and ready for the flight ahead. The flight checks were read out to Andrew by 'Biggles' McCarthy; brakes on; mixture rich; radiator covers closed; and so on until the checks were carried out and every detail was checked as being 'on line'.

A signal from the pilot and the ground crew connected the trolley acc (a series of batteries, also called accumulators, on a trolley designed to turn over and start each of the four Merlin engines) and each engine was started in turn, slowly, so slowly turning over until, belching smoke from the exhausts they roared into life, their pulsating heart sending vibrations through the airframe and through each crew member's body. Once the engines were up and running it was time for the ground crew to move away from the Lancaster to the nearby grass standing area, where, just a few moments ago they sat waiting to carry out the final tasks to get 'G' George and its crew into the air and away. Their job would be over for now, until, waiting patiently for many hours, they would look up into the sky for the first signs of returning aircraft seeking out for their bomber and its crew's safe return.

Each of the four Merlin V-12 liquid cooled engines guzzled petrol to keep the aircraft in the air. But not only petrol, oil in vast quantities was needed to prevent the engines from seizing up, in fact each engine had a 70 gallon oil tank, most of which would be used during each operation. Keeping a Lancaster flying was a very expensive business! These four massive engines would carry the Lancaster, its crew and bomb load to the Third Reich at some 270 mph (434 kph) and fly at a maximum ceiling of 21,500 feet (6,557 m). And not just to Germany. With a range of 1,160 miles it could reach even further afield.

Taxiing into its allotted take off position, 'G' George sat at the end of the runway waiting for the green flare or the coded flashing of a torch which would indicate that now was the time to start rolling along the concrete runway, take off and set course to the heart of the Third Reich. The signal finally came. With 'Biggles' McCarthy assisting Andrew at the controls, together they pushed the four throttle levers forward to their stops, unleashing the powerful Merlin's into life. The noise and vibration reverberated through the Lancaster, and slowly, so slowly at first, the massive weight of the bomber started to move along the concrete runway. While 'Biggles' kept a sharp look out monitoring the array of instruments on the panel in front of him he was also calling out the air speed to Andrew; "30 knots, 40 knots, 50 knots, rotate now." Andrew began pulling the control column back into his stomach to get 'G' George up into the air where she was designed to be. Reluctantly at first, the heavy bomber would not let go of its grip from Mother Earth, but then, as if it now realised that the four Merlins would win she let go her hold, surrendering to the power of the engines. The Lancaster suddenly lifted off from the concrete, rising up into the air, moving upwards and away from its base on its way to Germany. "Wheels up." Andrew called out. Immediately 'Biggles' operated the switch to raise the undercarriage. With a resounding thump the undercarriage folded the two massive wheels into the wings so reducing the aircraft's drag, which in turn increased the bombers air speed and lift. They were on their way now and nothing, apart from a major technical problem, would stop them.

Taking off was one of the most dangerous parts of any flight. An engine failure at that stage would probably mean the death of all on board and any unfortunate civilian or ground crew members. Fully laden with bombs and high octane aviation fuel, if the crew could not get their stricken bomber safely down onto the runway or other suitable landing area, then the bomber would crash, its deadly cargo exploding on impact.

Once England had been left behind and they were over the North Sea each air gunner would ask permission - if the pilot had not already ordered them - to test fire their .303 machine guns. In turn all would fire off a few rounds and report back to the pilot that all was well.

It would be getting quite dark now unless the night bombers 'natural' enemy - the Moon - was illuminating the night sky, with the risk that they would be clearly visible to any marauding German night fighters. This was the time when the crew's eyes, especially the gunners, would be roving the night sky to a set pattern, seeking out any sign of the enemy, looking for that small area of the surrounding darkness that might be darker than the natural night sky indicating the presence of a stalking night fighter. And if they should spot an enemy night fighter they then had to decide what action to take. If they were not the subject of the night fighter's interest the 'spotter' would warn the pilot and other gunners as to its position and they would hold their fire. Gunners would not open fire on an enemy aircraft unless they were certain they were being stalked by it. One thing this crew or any other crew would not want to do was to draw the enemies' attention to their aircraft if it wasn't necessary by firing their guns giving any marauding night fighters its location by the gun flashes!

Crossing the coast of Holland following the course laid down by the navigator, 'flak' - anti-aircraft fire also sometimes called 'ack-ack' - was another danger to be added to the risk of being shot down by night fighters. But they were lucky so far on this trip. No night fighter activity and the 'flak' was firing some miles away from them at some other unfortunate crew who appeared to be some miles off course and were probably flying quite alone in the vast expanse of sky. A huge explosion suddenly lit up the sky. The 'flak' had found its target. It must have been a direct hit. The bomb load exploding and totally destroying the other bomber. Its crew would have had no chance whatsoever to bail out, unless they had already been ordered to do so by their skipper fearing the worst. If no such order had been given and the crew was unaware of the serious damage sustained to their aircraft then they would still be at their stations. The chances of being able to successfully bail out of a damaged bomber, spiralling down to earth and possibly inverted were less than one in ten.

'G' George continued relentlessly on its way. The crew each prayed that somebody had managed somehow to get out of the stricken bomber in time, each of them reflecting silently on what they had just witnessed. It was 'Pop' who spoke first. "There but for the grace of God! Must have been a green crew to have been so far off of course boys. They wouldn't have known anything about it thankfully." Did they know the crew? They could have been drinking with them only the night before down at the 'Dog and Duck'. If a new or 'green' crew could survive their first three or four operations, or 'ops', then their chances of surviving a full tour - 30 ops - greatly improved. They would gel as a team and gain experience that would make the difference between life and death.

"OK. That's enough now. Don't communicate unless you have anything to report. We're over occupied Europe now so keep radio silence unless its urgent, OK boys?" Our pilot was correct of course, and his crew knew it. Only use the intercom if you had sometime important to report, and they must remember to speak clearly and precisely.

Heavy flak in the distance indicated where other bombers were dropping their bomb load, the exploding bombs could clearly be seen. No enemy night fighters had yet shown up so perhaps they were waiting in the wings to attack the bomber stream on its return. German night fighter pilots would avoid the target area while their flak guns were operating.

"Target approaching skipper." It was Arthur Baker speaking. "OK navigator, Thanks. 'Pop' take up your position now please. Give me corrections on the bomb run if you will 'Pop'." Andrew's voice was calm and relaxed as he now relied on 'Pop' Grey to guide the bomber ever closer to the target. "Left, left, steady, steady, hold it there. Left a bit more - just a touch." The TI's dropped by the Oboe equipped Mosquitoes were a great help in locating the precise point in which to release the bombs onto the target several thousand feet below. "That's it! Now steady, steady. Bombs gone!!" Immediately the bombs dropped out of the bomb bay the Lancaster gave a lurch and could be felt to lift upwards into the rarefied air. With the bombs no longer adding to the weight of the bomber it would shoot up into the night sky, climbing several hundred feet in a matter of seconds, something which all of the crew would feel. Rather like being in a lift as it suddenly and un-expectedly dropped down the lift shaft.

Once over the target and with its bombs dropped onto the target far below Andrew put the Lancaster into a pre-arranged 360-degree turn for the long trip home. Pre-arranged because all the Lancasters in the bomber stream would carry out the same manoeuvre to cut down the risk of mid-air collisions. With hundreds of aircraft over the target in the bomber stream the risk of collision was always great. A pilot would always know when there was another bomber close in front of him. Its prop wash would be felt on the following aircraft, making the pilot fight hard at the controls to keep his aircraft straight and level. Unfortunately there would be little or no warning if another bomber rose up from underneath to collide with you. And with bombs being dropped from other aircraft flying higher than you there was always the risk of these crashing through any lower flying aircraft. All of these reasons were why each squadron had a designated time over the target and a height to fly and bomb at

The mission had gone exactly as planned, and for once the weather forecast was spot on. Scanning the sky around him for other Lancasters' returning to base, Andrew could see none. He felt assured by that, for if he couldn't see any aircraft then any enemy night-fighter probably couldn't see his bomber either.

"OK everybody. We're on our way home. Keep a good look out now. No relaxing just yet. Still plenty of 'flak' to get through. And watch out for night fighters trying to get into the stream and follow us back to base. They've been joining the circuit lately and shooting up Lancasters while landing, not very sporting of them at all chaps!"

Moving rapidly away from the target now, the Lancaster flew much lighter. It had used up the best part of its fuel and it no longer carried the burden of its bomb load, and with a following wind, home and safety was just a few hours away.

Relaxing slightly he felt that his bomber and his crew in 'G' George should be fairly safe by now, as the ever probing searchlights and radar controlled anti aircraft fire of the Ruhr Valley rapidly disappeared behind it. Nonetheless he told his crew to be on the lookout for any marauding night-fighters that might still be intent on destroying any unfortunate lone or damaged bomber.

But 'G' George and its crew was soon to discover that the German defences had not yet given up their determination to destroy them for their audacity in attacking the Third Reich, something which Hermann Goering, as Commander in Chief of the much feared and vaunted Luftwaffe, had recklessly claimed would never happen.

Tracer bullets suddenly flashed past the cockpit, eagerly seeking out the bomber and its crew. Before Andrew could take any evasive action, the cannon shells from a Luftwaffe night fighter, probably a Me 110, were ripping along the port wing and into the Lancaster's now almost empty but highly volatile fuel tanks; almost empty but still full of highly combustible petrol vapour! Andrew corkscrewed violently with all the skill of a veteran pilot in a vain attempt to escape from the attacker but to no effect. The enemy aircraft was like a limpet, refusing to be thrown off. The German pilot was obviously an 'ace' and extremely determined to bring down the bomber and record yet another 'kill'. Why hadn't the pilot received any warning from 'Tiny' Watson to take evasive action? He was already dead or dying in the rear turret being the first victim of the attack. German night fighter crews knew that that they only had to eliminate the rear gunner and the bomber is totally defenceless from an attack beneath the fuselage. Using their upward firing 20mm cannon they could fire into the now defenceless aircraft without fear of any return fire.

Violently throwing the Lancaster into spiral dives and other defensive measures, Andrew just could not shake off the attack of the night fighter pilot who was determined to destroy not only the bomber but also its crew. Another attack and yet more well aimed cannon shells found their target as they thudded into the Lancaster's port engines which immediately exploded into a mass of flames spreading back along the side of the fuselage clearly illuminating the Lancaster's serial letters and RAF roundel. 'Biggles', as flight engineer, was frantically operating the fire extinguisher in the engine in a vain effort to put the fires out.

Yet more shells tore into the cockpit as the German pilot pressed home his attack, ripping it apart, several shells hitting 'Biggles' McCarthy in the head killing him instantly. Yet more shot the instrument panel into a thousand pieces, glass and metal splinters flying around to cut through the flesh of the crew. The bomber's controls were now very heavy and unresponsive as vital control cables and hydraulic pipes were severed by the cannon shells, making it impossible for Andrew to recover from the spiralling dive that the bomber was now in. There was no other option, at any second the bomber would dive into the ground where old Isaac Newton was beckoning. Andrew ordered his crew to bail out. He would follow once he had given them time to jump while he tried desperately to control the stricken bomber on its way down to the German countryside. But he knew all too well that attempting to jump from the bomber while it was diving and spiralling so violently would be practically impossible for them, but he must give them that one in a thousand chance. The members of the crew that were still alive after the attack and were able to bail out would have been thrown about inside the now earthward bound Lancaster. The effects of centrifugal force and disorientation would have made it extremely difficult, if not impossible, for any of them to reach their parachutes and then having clipped them on, to reach the exits of their stricken bomber to bail out. The odds were not in their favour, and they all knew it.

But one crewmember did make it. The Lancaster's pilot, Andrew Harper. He was able to make his escape out of his crippled bomber. By some miracle he managed to reach his parachute, and strapping it on he literally 'fell out' of the doomed bomber through the fuselage side where cannon shells had virtually ripped open the paneling. Somehow, instinctively pulling the ripcord to open his 'chute, he found himself falling through the cold night air. The sudden tug of the canopy opening jolted through his body. He was, for the moment, safe. Slowly drifting down to the dark earth below he was able to watch his faithful old Lancaster bomber plummet to the earth and explode in a massive ball of flame.

Only a few minutes could have passed from when they were first attacked by the night fighter. Where was it now? Was the pilot circling somewhere above him to confirm his 'kill'? Andrew hoped that one of his gunners had at least managed to get a few rounds off at him. The silence as he gently floated to earth was unreal. A few minutes ago they all believed they were safely on their way back to England, but he now found himself about to land into the very heart of the Third Reich. He hoped that he had at least managed to hold the Lancaster steady for just long enough for some of his crew to bail out in time.

Looking towards the crash site he attempted to steer himself as close as he could to be within easy reach of his burning Lancaster. The explosion and subsequent fires illuminated the ground to show that 'G' George had crashed in a fairly densely wooded area. Looking down he could see that he was rapidly approaching the treetops. Now to pray to God for a safe landing and that Lady Luck was on his side.

What follows is his remarkable story…

Chapter 2

Survival and Evasion

With the sharp cracking sound of snapping branches fading, I found myself lying in several feet of wind blown snow at the base of a tall pine tree. The parachute lines were tangled around my body with the canopy caught up in some of the lower branches. I was very lucky to have survived the descent. I knew that I had bailed out at a fairly low level and that my parachute could have barely had enough time to open. The branches and soft snow must have broken my fall, the pine branches slowing me down and then supporting me through the final fifty or so feet.

Quickly gathering my thoughts I could see just a short distance away the remains of my Lancaster which was burning fiercely, its wings and fuselage spread out over a large area as it broke up when crashing to earth. The flames were lighting up the trees and sky a vivid blood red colour. Several of the trees were also engulfed in flames, crackling and exploding as the resin within them ignited, caused no doubt by fuel from the ruptured wing tanks. How lucky I was to have survived.

Except for this sound everywhere was bathed in silence. As I lay here I instinctively looked up and listened for the

German night fighter that shot us down, but there was only an eerie silence, silence that is, apart from my heavy, panting breath and wildly beating heart. The night fighter pilot, happy with his night's work would be miles away by now searching the night sky for his next luckless victim.

Freeing myself from the tangle of parachute lines my next thought was for my crew. I prayed that some of them, if not all, had managed to escape and bail out to safety. I felt no obvious pain of broken bones, and so un-clipping my parachute harness I extradited myself from the broken tree branches and giving myself the 'once over' to ensure that I was, as far as I could tell, injury free, I managed to struggle through the deep snow drifts towards the crash site. Pausing I retrieved my whistle from inside my tunic and gave a good few resounding blasts on it to attract any other survivors. I waited and listened intently hoping and praying that somebody would respond in the same manner. But nothing, not a reply or any other response, no shouting for help or anything.Moving on I made my way to the wreck site. After what seemed a lifetime of struggling through the thick undergrowth and snow I eventually came upon the wreckage. The scene before me was one of total devastation. Fuel from the Lancaster had set fire to many of the trees that were already fiercely burning and spreading the fire further afield. The Lancaster's fuselage was miraculously still mainly intact although I could see that the port wing and both of its engines were separated from it, lying at a grotesque angle amongst the pines. But what of my crew? Did any of my friends manage to bail out? I could not recall seeing any other parachutes in my descent, but that didn't mean that nobody else had escaped in time. If I was lucky to escape then why not the others?

Exploding .303 bullets made me quickly drop to the ground. At first I thought that the local German militia had already arrived at the scene and were firing on me, but then I realised that they could not have possibly arrived here so quickly. The last thing I wanted now was to be hit by a stray bullet from my own aircraft and be injured, or killed. I carefully searched the undergrowth, pulling away broken branches and pulling aside small pieces of the Lancaster where I was able. I kept calling out above the noise of the exploding ammunition the names of my crew, but deep down inside of me I knew that it would be in vain. If they hadn't managed to bail out I knew that there was no hope that they could possibly have survived inside the Lancaster. But I must keep looking, just in case. They were my friends. We had grown into a tight knit unit and I couldn't let them down now.

I moved around to the other side of the wreckage shielding my face with my hands from the intense heat. This part of the fuselage was torn open like a can of sardines, exposing everything inside. What I found there was my very worst fear. Lying alongside the fuselage and still clearly visible despite the destruction were the rest of my crew. There was no movement or noise from any of them; it was evident that they were all dead. Nobody could possibly have survived the crash. I was the sole survivor. All my dear friends who had flown so many missions with me were now gone. I hoped and prayed that they did not suffer in their last moments on earth. In my minds eye the vision of 'Biggles' dying in front of me suddenly appeared as if in a nightmare.

I frantically attempted to enter the burning fuselage but to no avail. The heat and the still exploding bullets from the turret guns drove me back. There was no point anyhow, I knew they were all dead, but I just had to try. They were all gone. My friends who I had got to know so well over the past months, becoming a second family to me, Arthur Baker, 'Biggles' McCarthy, Bill Edney, 'Pop' Grey, 'Woody' and 'Tiny' Watson, all of them had gone. I shall never forget any of them, ever, for as long as I live.

I recited the one prayer that I could remember from my school days - the Lord's Prayer. Kneeling down in the now melting snow I slowly and quietly spoke the words over their bodies. There was nothing else I could do here. My concern now was to make my escape as best I could, for it wouldn't be too long until the local militia and police from any nearby town or village would find their way here to search for and capture any survivors. I knew exactly what the German civilians regarded shot down Royal Air Force bomber crews as - 'terror bombers.' If caught I hoped that my captors would be members of the German Army or local police. Civilians who had captured shot down Allied bomber crews had been known to take their revenge on them by severely beating them up. Some of the crews were publicly lynched by whatever means the German civilians could find, usually from the nearest tree or lamppost with no recrimination from the authorities who turned a blind eye to their illegal actions. If we had been shot down over Belgium, France or Holland the chances of escaping back to England would have been far better. We were given lectures in England by other successful escapees - Allied air-crew who had made that 'home run' - about evasion tactics and who we should contact and trust in the event of being shot down. But I was in German territory, the enemies' homeland. I couldn't contact or trust anybody. Everyone had to be regarded as my enemy.

I calculated that as we were still heading east away from the target before turning onto a southerly course for our planned course home that we had crashed somewhere south of Munich near to the Austrian border and east of Switzerland. If only I could evade capture and make my way to the safety of neutral Switzerland. Reluctantly moving away from the wreckage - I felt an intense guilt about leaving my friends behind - I retreated into the darkness finding a spot where I could check my escape pack; all aircrews carried this vital piece of equipment for just such a situation. A miniature compass together with a silk map of Europe, Horlicks tablets, some very hard biscuits plus glucose tablets and chocolate bars, water purifying tablets and Benzedrine energy tablets. Not much to sustain me, but that is all I had. I regret now that I didn't make up my own pack for just such an emergency as this, but wouldn't that have been tempting fate? Some of my fellow pilots on the squadron even carried their own civilian clothing in a small rucksack for just such an event. To my mind that exposed them to being classed as spies or saboteurs if caught in civilian clothing while on the run. The only two pieces of advise I took any notice of from other escapees who had made that 'home run' back to England was not to grow a moustache for if bailing out over France this was a dead give way as no young Frenchmen wore them. The Germans would arrest and question any man they came across who was sporting one; and I didn't wear the thick white woollen jumper that most other crews wore. Although nice and warm to wear these weren't fashionable in France, or any other European country, and they too would have been a give away and attract the attention of the enemy.

I checked my compass and estimated my direction of travel. Safely gathering up my escape kit I headed in the direction that would, I hoped, eventually bring me to the Swiss frontier - as long as I could keep clear of my pursuers. Deciding that it would only be safe to travel by night and lay low during the day, I started off, but not before I gave a last look back to my old friends. I just hoped that the Germans would treat their remains with the respect that they all deserved.

So this was to be my next mission. My battle to somehow reach England and then to get back into the war! I headed off and immediately my first problem appeared behind me - I would be leaving a very easy trail to follow in the snow! I prayed to God, just hoping that the now steadily falling snow would quickly cover my tracks before my pursuers arrived and spotted my footprints. Setting off I desperately tried to remember all that we had been taught at our evasion lectures in the event of actually coming down into enemy held territory.

What was it our instructor had said to us? "Try to keep cheerful to keep your mind positive, and use sound common sense." That was one tip. What were the others? They could be lifesavers now. If only I could remember them. "Save your energy and carefully ration the contents of your food pack. Be careful of drinking foul water from dubious sources - use the sterilising pack. Benzedrine (for energy) - use it wisely and follow the instructions on the pack. Feet! They are your way back to your own lines and safety - look after them! Dry your socks whenever you can and if shot down during wintertime be alert for the first signs of frostbite - blackening toes and fingers. Sleep when and where you can for as long as you can. A mind starved of sleep will make irrational and possibly dangerous decisions. Keep close to hedges where you can quickly gain shelter if anybody approaches you on the road, and never ever walk on the sky line or walk in the centre of open fields, you will be easily spotted by searchers and make a good target if they should decide to fire upon you first and then ask questions later. Use Old Mother Nature, she offers you the best protection by using her natural camouflage to conceal yourself. Look after what equipment you have - watches and a compass need to be protected and secured in a safe place on your person. If you should misplace your compass, remember that dawn is in the east and sunset in the west. At night if the sky is clear use the North Star for guidance. As for food, remember that all animals in Europe are edible - even rats, mice & snails, so with common sense there is no real need to go hungry!"

So much to try to remember, but if I am to evade the enemy I must put all of this, and more, into practice, after all, our instructor had successfully made that 'home run' so he gave us his knowledge which he had gained by experience.

I estimated that it must be some 200 miles to the Swiss frontier. In these conditions I calculated that being able to walk 20 miles each night - we had been told at the lectures that night time travel was far safer than travelling during the day - over very rough and hilly terrain, it would take me at least 10 days to reach Switzerland and safety - but then I had the problem of crossing the frontier which was bound to be very well patrolled and guarded - why didn't those lectures give any information about coming down in German territory! I resolved to correct that omission on my return, and I was determined that I would return. I put these negative thoughts out of my head, I must stay positive if I was to reach England and continue my part in the war.

But I must get to Switzerland first and it was not going to be easy, of that I had no illusions. Food, shelter and keeping warm and dry would be my first requirements if I were going to succeed. My escape rations of chocolate, biscuits and Horlicks tablets would not last me for too long, so I would have to steal what food I could from any outlying farms and trust to luck - and there would have to be lots of luck - that I would not be discovered. I was in enemy territory where everyone was against me and would be on the look out for me. The news of an escaping airman would soon be broadcast around the countryside, and there was also a standing reward offered for the capture of any Allied aircrew escapee - dead or alive!

Farm dogs would be a major problem. I had to be extremely careful in foraging for food or shelter near to farms so as not to disturb them, as their barking would undoubtedly give my presence away to any farmer who would surely alert the military and police. I must also assume that he wouldn't investigate any disturbance unarmed. I remember clearly from my childhood times working during the school holidays on our local farm that the farmer had at least one shotgun at hand to shoot rabbits and other vermin. This time however I would be the target and not the rabbits! Shelter during the day from the cold and snow could be a major problem. Any shelter had to be secure from prying eyes and as comfortable as I could make it to hopefully get ample sleep. Failing to find a safe refuge in a farmer's barn or shed to hide up in during the daytime I could always make a shelter from any fallen tree branches and conceal myself in the thick undergrowth. And I had one consolation; it would probably be as difficult for my pursuers in this weather as it was going to be for me!

Every footstep became an exhausting effort as I slowly plodded my way through the fairly deep snow and I was soon sweating quite freely. After about an hour of hard and difficult trudging I came across what appeared to be a regularly used cart track. In the moonlight I could clearly see that farm carts and the feet of many farmers had packed the snow hard so it would be far easier for me to put some distance between myself and my pursuers. Standing there for a while I decided to take a big risk and walk along it as far as I could, hoping that my footprints would blend in and be indistinguishable from the tracks of the cart horses and carts, and anyway, the falling snow would soon obscure them. Checking my compass I turned right onto the track as that appeared to take me in the general direction I wanted to travel. The going was now much easier if a lot more dangerous, but I was banking that there would be nobody else out and about at this time of the night - not just yet anyway! But I still had to be alert just in case any locals were using the track as well, returning from visiting fellow farmers or the local hostelry, after all I didn't know if the track led from a farm and on to the farmer's fields, or was a minor road between villages. I pressed steadily on being fairly safe in the knowledge that I had the track to myself until daybreak.

Walking steadily now for a couple of hours, I stumbled across what appeared to be a woodman's shed in a small clearing to one side of the track. It was still night and too early to seek shelter, so I decided to investigate and see if there was anything inside which could prove to be of some use to me. Making as little noise as I could - I didn't know how near the owner's house or farm might be - I easily forced the old wooden door open and entered the shed where I discovered, much to my joy, an old heavy overcoat and some well worn boots. I took the overcoat from the nail it was hanging from and wore it over my flying suit; it was a snug, if not a too tight fit. The old, well-worn leather boots replaced my flying boots that had now become saturated with melted snow and very cumbersome and heavy. I regretted disposing of these, for although when dry they kept out the cold, they had become so sodden and heavy that they made walking very difficult and all but impossible. The old boots reached up to my knees and hopefully would keep the wet snow out and fortunately, being far too big for my feet; I was still able to wear my thick woollen socks inside of them. Whoever the owner of the coat and boots was he must have been quite a size, I just hoped that I didn't bump into him! Although my socks were wet, they at least helped to insulate my feet and legs from the cold until I could hope to dry them out when I rested up for the coming day. Lady Luck was still with me. I felt a lot happier now and my spirits rose. The overcoat would give me the appearance of, I hoped, a tramp, and if the worst did happen and I was caught I still had my flying suit beneath it to prove beyond any doubt that I was in fact a shot down airman and as such I was protected by the Geneva Convention.

I hid my flying boots and searched the shed for anything else which I could make use of. I discovered tucked away in a corner some sacks with what appeared to be turnips or swedes inside, stored presumably to feed the cattle which grazed here during the spring and summer months in the open fields which I could now see running alongside the forest edge. Stuffing the pockets of my newly 'liberated' coat I could feast on these and together with the chocolate and biscuits from my escape pack could make a palatable meal. Things were looking much better now and I became quite elated. I felt that if my luck could hold out like this I might yet make a home run and return to England.

Securing the shed door as best I could in case my entry should be spotted and whereabouts discovered, I shuffled silently away with my booty. Feeling more secure now, as I was sure that I could pass as a local going about his business if I should be spotted.

I was making good time and several more hours passed before I realised that dawn had begun to break and it was starting to get light. I decided that I had to get off of the track to a safer location and find a hide-away for the day so I quickly retreated back into the deep folds of the forest. It was fortunate for me that the ground under the tall pines was fairly sparse of snow so as not to leave too much of a trail of footprints behind me to disclose my hiding place for the coming day. Scouring through the dense undergrowth an ideal spot was soon found. A large thicket of thorn and bramble bushes surrounded by immature trees. If I could just force my way into the middle of the bramble thicket I could rest there in some security until nightfall. Searching around the perimeter of the brambles I soon found a way in. Foxes or some other wild animal had already shaped a low tunnel into the centre, so I crawled in on my hands and knees. To hide all signs of my entry I used a few twigs and carefully 'brushed' over my footprints to hopefully hide them from all but the most closest scrutiny. I pushed and pulled the brambles to one side and as I made my way through to the centre I carefully replaced them behind me to disguise the tunnel. The thought that whatever wild beast had made this their refuge in the first place didn't occur to me until I had managed to crawl for about twenty feet into a fairly clear patch in the very middle where the brambles had all but died away. Who would have the biggest surprise I wondered, me or the returning animal! This was a Godsend and considering everything much better than I could have ever hoped for. I could at least curl up here, and I was sure I could not be spotted! I carefully cleared twigs and branches away to make a bigger patch large enough for me to be able to lie down and be comfortable. The branches and stems I had moved were repositioned around my little 'sanctuary' to disguise it even more from the outside world, I even managed to pull some of the longer stems and branches over the top of me to form a roof of sorts. This I hoped would not only hide me from any prying eyes but also help to keep the worst of any snow fall off of me and of course, give my hideout an even more natural appearance. Making myself as comfortable as I could I reached into my jacket pocket and I retrieved one or two of the turnips. Cleaning the worst of the dirt off of them I took a big bite from one. A bit 'stringy' and with quite a strong sweet taste, but beggars can't be choosers as they say! The two squares of chocolate that I allowed myself afterwards helped to get rid of the strong earthen taste the turnip had left in my mouth. Melting some snow in my cupped hands, I took my first 'drink' since leaving my base in England for what now seemed to be in another life. That was followed by one of the Horlicks and glucose tablets. What a veritable feast! I settled down afterwards, again checking that my entrance into the brambles looked undisturbed, satisfying myself that it was as good as I could make it. Finding the old overcoat was a tremendous stroke of luck. I could button it up right up to my neck, and its deep, wide collar almost covered my face keeping my ears insulated from the cold air. I curled up, my knees and legs tucked underneath the deep folds of the overcoat in an attempt to retain as much body heat as I could. Feeling safer now, I closed my eyes and quickly fell into an exhausted sleep.

I must have slept soundly for several hours. The sun was quite high overhead and the winter warmth from it felt good on my face. I slowly roused myself. Every joint and muscle in my body screamed in rebellion to the sudden movements I was forcing it to make. Eventually managing to sit upright I very carefully and slowly poked my head out of the top of the protection of the brambles after listening carefully for any signs of human activity. There must have been a heavy snowfall during the night, for I was covered in a sprinkling of it although most had settled on top of my 'roof' of branches. At any other time this would have reminded me of my home in Lincolnshire where my wife and young son would by now have been told by my Commanding Officer and the camp padre that I was 'overdue' and listed as 'missing in action'. I hoped that somebody - a neighbour or wife of one of the other crews that we knew - would be there to console her and give her the strength to believe that I could still be alive. All service wives and mothers hope that they will never receive this kind of news, but as there was no definite news that I had been killed there was hope. Once the International Red Cross had been informed as to my status - either a prisoner of war, killed or missing in action - by the German authorities, my wife would be in a state of limbo until the information was passed on. God bless the Red Cross and the Geneva Convention, which gave protection to prisoners of war, provided of course, that their individual countries had 'singed' up to it. Fortunately Great

Britain and Germany had, but the Soviet Union hadn't so their PoWs were given no protection at all by the Geneva Convention.

Only a few hours had passed since I was shot down but it seemed as if I had been on 'the run' for ages. I wondered if the Germans had discovered the wreckage of faithful old 'G' George. They must surely have done so by now. And my crew, my friends with whom I would have drinks with at our local pub? I prayed to God that the Germans had found their bodies and were treating them with the respect they deserved.

How far had I travelled this first night, probably no more than 10 or 12 miles at the most? Was I far enough away from the crash site? How far afield would the Germans extend their search area? With these questions still whirling around inside of my very fuzzy head I curled up to get some more sleep and rest until nightfall. I was glad for my heavy flying suit and newly acquired coat; at least they kept the worst of the cold at bay. If I could only get through today alright I really felt that my chances of reaching England would improve The longer I was at liberty then surely the search for me must be relaxed and finally called to a halt; the Germans may even come to the conclusion that I had perished in the wreckage but that my body could not be found. I felt a lot better thinking that and believed that 'Lady Luck' was keeping her eyes on me like a guardian angel.

I fell into a deep sleep, dreaming about my wife and young son back in Lincolnshire. It felt so real to me, almost as if I only had to reach out and I could touch them. They were in my mother's garden, playing together in the gloriously warm sun. I could see the colour of my wife's hair, shimmering as the sun's rays caught it. My son was crawling on the green, freshly mown grass, trying to catch passing butterflies that gently flew silently from flower to flower. Coming from the old thatched cottage was the laughter of my mother as she watched her grandson in his vain attempts to reach them, his tiny fingers opening and closing as he tried to grasp them. Then, in an instant, I was transported to my Lancaster, fighting the controls again, desperately trying to keep her in the air. I could hear the cannon shells, the smell of burning fabric and fuel; the fire that was trying to consume me; smoke filled my nostrils and lungs until I felt I was suffocating. I could clearly see the faces of my crew before me now. Each of them slowly fading and disappearing, becoming invisible even as I looked upon them. "I must get out, I must get out." I shouted over and over again, struggling to get away from the destruction and death that surrounded me.

It was the sound of heavy footsteps crunching in the snow and men shouting to each other that quickly woke me up and brought my thoughts back to reality. Immediately my whole cold and aching body tensed up. My mind was in a frenzied whirl. Had I been discovered? Had I really shouted out in my dream? Did I replace every bramble and branch back in place to look as natural as possible? Was the light falling of snow through the night enough to cover my tracks? These and a thousand other worrying doubts leapt into my mind. Keeping perfectly still even though my body was suffering from cramped and half frozen muscles, I tuned my ears to try and discover what was happening. More shouting and calling out! I was being hunted. They must have discovered the broken door on the hut and obviously roused the owner to discover if anything had been taken. He would of course realise that the overcoat and boots were missing and report this to the searchers who would instantly realise that the missing crewmember they were searching for must have taken them. I began to violently tremble and shake, whether caused by the cold or fear of being discovered, or both, I wasn't sure. The shouting came steadily closer. I laid down as low as I could, trying to bury my body in the dead leaves and moss that surrounded me, trying to become invisible to any prying eyes that might look into my hideout.

The shouting began to die down as if moving away from me. Daring to look up I peered through the cover of the brambles towards the path. There he was! No more than thirty feet away from my hiding place. My first encounter with the enemy. Flying to targets in Nazi Germany at 20,000 feet makes this war very impersonal. You don't see the enemy or feel just what it must be like to have tons of high explosive dropped on top of you. But this brought the reality, the face of war, right up and very close. A German soldier carrying his rifle at the ready - and looking straight towards me. I forced myself to slowly and silently crouch much lower for the protection of the ground and surrounding brambles. Had I been discovered? He made no sign of having seen me; he was just standing there as if he sensed something was amiss. Surely if he had spotted me he would have called for help and alerted his comrades? That is what I would have done. He hesitantly came a few steps closer, much closer now. I could just make out through the brambles the bayonet attached to his rifle, glinting menacingly in the winter sun. "Keep perfectly still now" I mentally told myself. "Mustn't make a movement." I held my breath in case the condensation gave my position away. He appeared to relax slightly. The rifle that he was holding so aggressively was now slung over his shoulder. Reaching into his greatcoat pocket he pulled out a packet of cigarettes, and, lighting one, took several deep 'drags' from it before flicking it carelessly away. After taking one last visual search and apparently being satisfied, he moved away down the path. I was safe, for the moment anyway. I wish he had tossed his cigarette in my direction! What I would have given for a few puffs from it. I felt myself strangely actually feeling quite sorry for him. He didn't give me the impression of being one of Germany's elite, much-feared super race. With a clear paunch under his greatcoat, and a definite stooping of the shoulders, this was not one of the Wermachts' finest. He was probably a local Home Guard who was dragged out of his comfortable, warm bed last night, away from his loving Frau and ordered to search this area of wood. All he wanted to do was to get his designated area checked as quickly as possible, report 'nothing found' and then return to the comforting arms of his loving wife, who was probably just as annoyed at her husband being called out to search for me as he was.

The whole incident must have lasted no more than four or five minutes, but in that short time I had mentally aged years. My body started to relax, I again began shaking violently, and convulsions ran through every aching muscle, I felt as if I was about to be violently sick, not through fear but the relief of not being discovered. The shock of being so nearly found out and captured was playing havoc with my mind. The thought of coming that close to the enemy again filled me with fear, dread and despair. Would I be so lucky the next time? I tried to relax. I must try and rest for tonight's attempt to get nearer to the Swiss border and eventual freedom. I broke into another of my chocolate bars and took my last glucose tablet hoping that the sugar and energy from both would give me a much-needed boost. There was nothing I could do now until nightfall. Quietly snuggling down into the ground, wrapping the old coat around my body I drifted off into a half sleep, not daring to go into a deep sleep for fear of the Germans returning for another swoop through the woods, I may not be so lucky next time. Sleep came slowly, but I did sleep.

Waking up I felt surprisingly much better. Was it because I had had my first encounter with the enemy and had won? Knowing that the danger, for the time being at least, had safely passed me by. Night was now rapidly approaching and I must move on, forever on, to reach my goal. Rubbing my limbs and joints to get the circulation flowing, I carefully gathered my meagre rations together and checking that everything appeared to be clear, made my way out of my precious shelter. There had been another light fall of snow while I was asleep and I really needed to put some distance between my shelter and the crash site tonight. I decided to risk keeping to the footpath after checking my compass and finding that, for the moment anyway, the track was still heading in the direction I wished to travel. I just had to take the risk of travelling this way. The longer I was at out in the open the more opportunity there would be of the enemy catching me. I was determined to make as much progress as possible. Yes, I decided that it was worth the risk.

I stood silently on the track for a moment or two, listening for any sounds of human activity. Nothing. All was quiet except for the sound of a light breeze playing amongst the pine branches high above me.

I had already decided in my mind to walk at a steady yet constant pace to keep a natural rhythm in an effort to conserve energy. There were already clouds scurrying across the face of the moon, obscuring its helpful light that had been showing me the way safely forward. If it should disappear altogether then I could be in some difficulty when I needed to check my compass, for check it I must to ensure that I was travelling in the correct direction. To walk for what could be many miles only to discover that I had been heading the wrong way would be devastating. I knew my limitations. I had a meagre supply of food to sustain me, and exhaustion combined with lack of sleep would affect my mental ability to make rational decisions. To make such an error in navigation was just not acceptable.

I walked on. It was snowing again although thankfully, not too heavy. Making good time; I estimated I had been walking for about three or four hours and had travelled about 10 miles. The snow was falling much heavier now, and the wind was whipping it up into some fairly deep drifts where the pines ran alongside of the track, hindering my progress. The extra effort that I needed to make my way through them was making me sweat quite heavily, soaking my clothing under the overcoat. The cold was penetrating through to my flesh sending shivers through my body. I couldn't understand why this should be as I was sweating quite freely so I must be creating heat to keep myself warm. The realisation that I was in fact loosing body heat through the sweating suddenly dawned on me. This was no good at all. Loosing vital body heat and getting wetter with every step. Very soon I would develop hypothermia and that would be the end of me. I had to stop walking and find some shelter out of this worsening weather - and quickly! But where was I? I had no idea; I was totally lost. What a fool I had been. With no compass checks since I started out, I could have been walking around in circles following this track for all I knew! My silk map was of no use until I knew where I was so I could not yet plot a course to Switzerland. Shelter, I must find shelter, and quickly.

The sudden baying of a dog echoed in my ears. Where there were dogs there must be humans. Perhaps an isolated farm was nearby where I could find shelter and even food. I moved off in the direction that the barking was coming from, luckily it still seemed to take me along the track way. The barking was getting louder now, the noise carrying quite clearly in the cold night air.

Was that a light shining from ahead? Could it be? Yes, a light. I must take care now. Steadily and stealthily inching my way forward to its beckoning beacon, as I came nearer the silhouette of a farmhouse came into view. A door was opened allowing more light to fall onto the snow outside. A gruff Germanic voice was calling out into the darkness. A dog appeared from nearby, obviously the same one that had been barking. A yelp as the farmer gave the dog a kick, and then he was back inside no doubt to sit in front of a glorious warm log fire. The door was slammed shut and with more shouting the light was extinguished. The dog had obviously been locked out and was calling for his master to let him in out of this foul weather! What a wonderful stroke of luck. So old Lady Luck was still sitting on my shoulder. Waiting for as long as I dared and looking for any movement from within the farmhouse, I moved forwards, quietly, so quietly so as not to disturb and awaken either the dog or farmer to my presence. Crouching down in the courtyard I could see several sheds to one side of the main house. I moved towards the barn that was farthest away from the house, fortunately the doors had been left open. Even from where I stood I could smell hay, beckoning me in to feel the softness and warmth that it offered. My mind was made up. Moving forward I went in. Snow had been blown in onto the earthen floor. With the whiteness of the snow as a contract to the darkened interior I could dimly make out the shapes of numerous crates and small items of farming implements; rakes, spades and what appeared to be scythes, scattered about in no particular semblance of order. A wooden stepladder, which was propped up against the wall, caught my attention. Looking up into the gloom I could see what could only be a hayloft and sanctuary. I spun around in my tracks and checked that all was still quiet. I moved across to the ladder, hoping that it wouldn't be attached to the old wooden barn walls by ropes or nails. Grasping it firmly with both hands, I gingerly lifted it away from its resting place. It moved! Not daring to believe my good fortune I slowly and as quietly as I could moved it over to where I could lean it against the floor beams of the loft, taking great care not to fall over any tools lying on the floor. At last it was safely in place. Placing one foot onto the bottom rung I tested it to see if it would support my weight without giving way, my theory being that if this rung held my weight, then the others should also. It held. Slowly now I took each rung very carefully, my near frozen hands trembling with anticipation as I placed them on either side of the ladder. Treading on one rung at a time I inched my way to the top until I was standing amongst the hay that lay on the wooden floor. I collapsed into the hay, my breathing very laboured, I was gasping for breath. Should I leave the ladder where it was, or could I push my luck even further and lift it up into the loft with me, where it would be out of sight and could not be used by the farmer to gain access? Right or wrong I hauled it up alongside of me. The effort of doing this really pushed my remaining strength to its limit and beyond. I was totally exhausted, panting and shaking like a very old man instead of a fit twenty year old. Had I really aged that quickly over the last day or so? I was more physically and mentally exhausted than I realised. I knew now that if I hadn't come across this barn I would probably not have survived the night but would have frozen to death in the snowy wastes of the forest, my body lying where I had fallen waiting for somebody to discover it.

Outside the wind was really blowing now, much worse than it had been earlier. The snow was being carried into the barn, creating a drift several feet high. I needn't have any fears of my entry being discovered, any evidence of me being here would soon be covered over by the fast falling snow. Tiredness and exhaustion were fast over taking me now. Burrowing myself deep into the welcoming hay, insulated from the weather and everything else outside of my safe cocoon, I instantly fell into a deep sleep, certain that nobody would disturb me for several hours. Only a complete idiot - and escaping airmen - would contemplate venturing out in this vile weather!

Cramp from abused muscles woke me up. Stretching out I tried to coax them back into life. How long had I been soundly asleep I wondered? Lying there for a moment I listened out for any signs of activity. None, even the dog wasn't barking. Carefully pushing my head up through the depth of hay that I was buried under I saw before me the interior of the barn in bright daylight. Snow had built up in the doorway to a height of perhaps five or six feet, so nobody would find it easy to get through to the interior of the barn if they wanted to. The barn itself was constructed of timber and was plainly many years old. Spiders' webs and the dust of many years lay everywhere, in fact it appeared that nobody had been here for ages such was the extent of rubbish and discarded broken and rusted farming tools, there was even a dilapidated bicycle lying against the wall. What a pity the ground was covered in snow. I could possible have used this to cycle away!

These signs gave me encouragement. I considered that I was probably as safe here as in the vaults of the Bank of England! I could stay here and rest up until the weather improved and I had regained my strength enough to press on to Switzerland. But first I must get food, water and dry clothes from somewhere. Looking at my watch it was twelve minutes past four. It would be getting dark soon so if I was to found out more about my surroundings I should look now while there was still daylight. Perhaps I would find something of use in this old barn, after all, I had already discovered and liberated my overcoat and boots from that other barn.

Without further ado I left my refuge of the night and crawled over to the ladder. Lowering it quietly to the ground I carefully descended to the floor, the muscles and joints in my body still stiff, but functioning without rebelling too much against the movement. Once on the floor I again listened for any activity. None, so my search began. First I inspected the contents of the crates I had seen the previous night. Removing the lid of the first I was disappointed to find nothing but old hessian sacks. In disgust I replaced the lid and moved onto the next, trying to keep my boots out of the snow lest the imprint would give my incursion here away. This one held better prospects. It contained what appeared to be bottles of liquid of some kind, but what exactly? Picking one up I looked for a label but found none.

Nothing for it then but to open it up and carefully have a taste! Raising the bottle to my lips I silently prayed that the contents were not poison. I smelt it first, and then with both fingers crossed took a sip. Brandy! The bottle held brandy! This was indeed a treasure to find. Replacing the cork I put it to one side, now for some of the others. Sampling other bottles I was surprised to find that they all contained alcohol, either excellent tasting white wines, schnapps or more brandy. I selected a bottle of wine and schnapps to go with the brandy. If I was in the party mood I could really get drunk! The next two crates held nothing but bits of machinery parts and old magazines and newspapers.

A large wooden sea chest next caught my eye. It wasn't locked, but the heavy lid was quite a job to lift open, not because the hinges were rusted and stiff, but because I didn't have the strength to lift it as it was so heavy. Slowly using one arm to prise it open and the other to support it, it finally gave way and revealed its inner secrets. There were perhaps half a dozen large round objects that looked as if they were wrapped in a gauze material. And the smell. It was overwhelming, but not a foul smell, but rather one that reminded me of my childhood days helping out at one of our neighbouring farms where the farmer had a dairy herd. It was cheese! Slabs of the best smelling cheese I have ever smelt. My mouth began to water with just the thought of biting into one of these beautiful smelling delicacies. Lifting one out I was surprised as to its weight. I just hoped I could carry it up into my sanctuary along with the wine and other bottles I had selected. All I needed now was some good German bread to go with it.

It was now rapidly approaching nightfall; so further investigation would have to wait. I must retreat to the safety of the loft and settle in for the night, and what a night this was going to be. Retrieving one of the sacks I had discovered in the first crate, I carefully placed the bottles into it. They would be the first 'cargo' up the ladder. I would have to carry the cheese separately as it was far too heavy to be carried with the wine.

Once in the loft I pulled the ladder up behind me. Just in time as it was now completely dark so I had to use my senses to open the wine and break into the cheese for the best meal I have had since leaving England. Completely satisfied now, my stomach full with excellent cheese and washed down with an equally excellent German white wine, I had to look to taking stock of my physical shape and condition. Removing the old boots and my RAF issue thick woollen socks I felt my feet and toes with my hands, searching for any blisters or other such abrasions that needed to be looked at better in tomorrow's light of day. I was very relieved to find that my feet were only slightly swollen but no blisters. I left my feet bare, covering them in the sack that I had used for my booty. The socks I positioned near my body in an effort to use my body heat to dry them. I couldn't do much with the boots except hope they would dry out to some extent so I laid them out in an attempt to dry them in readiness for the next stage of my home run.

Now for the overcoat that had served me so well. Emptying the pockets of what remained of my escape kit and last turnip I took it off and placed it to one side. It had dried off whilst I had been asleep earlier, the heat from my body sufficient to dry it almost completely. My uniform was quite dry, it was quite amazing what the heat from my body was able to achieve while I slept. I settled down for the night, snug within the deep layers of straw. Tomorrow

I would investigate further afield. There had been no sign of any activity from the farmhouse, either from its human occupant that had opened the door last night or the dog that I had heard barking so loudly.

Waking early - it was just beginning to get light - I rubbed my limbs to encourage the blood to circulate. I had slept well again last night, the plentiful supply of alcohol no doubt helping! Rumblings from my stomach prompting me that I should have a meal before venturing out. Selecting a handy piece of cheese from my now replenished food supply, I tucked in until I could eat no more, then, washing it down with the last of an already opened bottle of wine I decided on my next move. I decided that night travel was out of the question now. I was lucky to find this shelter and the food and drink. I could so easily have wondered around in circles, exhausting myself until I could go no further. Regardless of what we had been told on our survival lectures, I would travel now during daylight, taking extra care and be on full alert. After all, I did have the appearance of a tramp now. My hair was unkempt, I needed a good shave and wash, and I knew I smelt rather badly! If I were approached I would walk with a hunch and drag a leg as if I was partially invalided. If spoken to then I would mumble something incoherently hoping that my questioner would not pursue their questions and let me go on my way, glad to see the back of me. That then, was my plan.

Taking stock of everything I decided that as I felt reasonably well and recovered that today I must move on. There would be no telling when the farmer and his dog would decide to come into the barn for some of the wine or cheese he had stored away and I certainly didn't want to be caught up here like a rat in a trap. I could see outside now that there had been no more snow overnight, although there must have been a good hard frost as parts of my shelter had a glittering sparkle of frost up near the joists of the roof. I packed everything together in the old sack; two full bottles of wine; a bottle of brandy; two of the cheeses, and lastly the remains of my last turnip. My woollen socks, which I had kept near to my body overnight to keep them warm, felt comforting against my feet and legs. The leather boots were slipped on and tied up nice and tight. Next came the overcoat. Wearing it over my uniform and buttoning it up as high as I could I felt ready to face the world again. Carefully positioning the ladder, I slung the sack with my bounty over my shoulder and quietly climbed down the steps for the last time. I stood silently for a moment, listening again for any sign of noise or movement of the farmer or his dog. Hearing nothing I ventured out into the farm yard, on the alert for them all of the time. That's odd, I thought to myself, no smoke coming from the chimneystack, surely he must have a good fire going in the house? I moved forward, steadily, a footstep at a time expecting to be challenged at any moment.

In the snow were clear tracks as if a sledge had been drawn along, and there, running in between where the sledge runners showed were the imprints of what could only have been a horse. No smoke from the chimney; no dog barking; and no noise. It could only mean one thing, the farmer had, at some time as I slept so soundly, left his farmhouse for whatever reason and taken his dog with him. What a stroke of luck. But how long ago did he leave, and when would he return from his trip? I had no way of answering these questions. Now a second thought exploded inside my head. Could I risk getting into his cottage somehow and see if I could find anything that would be of use to me? The door and windows looked securely fastened, each window was shuttered up and secured with a thick metal bar and lock. Thinking quickly, the wiser and rational thinking part of my brain said 'No'. To break-in in the hope of finding something useful was outweighed by the risk of being caught inside and not being able to make my escape. Perhaps there were more than two farmers living here? I would have no chance in trying to fight my way out in that case, and then there was the dog to contend with. No, I would go with what I already had and be thankful for it.

"Check the compass. Which way do I need to travel?" I said to myself, thinking more clearly now. Due south, that was to be my heading. With that I set off again. Would I be so lucky again tonight with finding shelter? Time would tell.

My course sent me into the forest and away from the cart track. Trudging through the sometimes knee deep snow I made slow progress. As I went deeper into the forest however the snow became less and less thick. Obviously the pine braches had caught most of what had fallen on their upper branches. I thought back to how these branches and the snow had probably saved my life a few days earlier when I had bailed out, the branches then held out their limbs as if they were so many strong arms trying to catch me and lower me down to earth safely.

Remembering to check my compass regularly I continued slowly but more steadily on my way. If only I knew exactly where I was, my silk map was no good at all. Without knowing my position I could not use it to try and pinpoint my whereabouts and then plot a route to Switzerland. Perhaps soon I would come across a road with a sign giving directions and distance to a nearby town. On and on I walked, stumbling from one pine to the next. Not a sign of life anywhere, was that good or bad? I considered this question to keep my brain active. Discussing the problem with myself I came to the conclusion that it was neither good nor bad! Good, because the absence of people made the chances of being found and captured less likely; bad, because I needed to know where I was, and for that I had to find the name of a town or better still, a road sign. But to find these also meant civilisation, people, dogs and the risk of capture.

During my subconscious discussion I had stumbled out of the forest and into the open without noticing! I was standing in open ground, on a hilltop, just one of the things we had been warned not to do. Shocked at this severe lapse in concentration I immediately dropped into the snow, shaking with the thought of how stupid I had been. There was far less snow here, so my dark overcoat must be standing out like a beacon in the wilderness of white snow, plain for any watching eyes to see. Inch by painful inch I slid back on my stomach to the shelter and safety of the pines. Listening intently above the beating of my heart and gasping breath, I could hear no shouts of alarm from below. Could I have been lucky and my presence not noticed? Peering up through the snow sprinkled branches I could make out in the valley below a small village, more of a hamlet really. Several of the tiny cottages had smoke, slowly whispering out into the cold, clear air, disappearing as if by magic, as the soft breeze took it away.

The events of these last few minutes had shaken me very badly. I said to myself, over and over again in my mind, "How stupid could I have been!" This was as far as I could go today. Looking at the winter's sun I calculated that it was well past midday, which my watch confirmed. I would find some shelter in these woods tonight, resting and deciding what my next course of action would be. I already knew that tomorrow I would have to risk going down to the village if I was to discover my whereabouts. Approaching the village by road was my best option. To walk out of this forest, across open fields would surely just draw attention to myself. It had to be from the road. But now to find shelter for the coming night. I retraced my footsteps back into the forest, all the time looking for a suitable shelter and keeping a listen out for any activity from the village just in case I had been observed. I noticed a ditch running off at a right angle across my path. Thinking that I could pull some twigs and branches over the top of it to form a shelter for the night I clambered, or rather slid, down into it. Making my way along it I came across a wooden bridge of sorts with a track running either side of it. This was my shelter I thought! I could burrow through the snowdrift and get into the centre of it where I was confident I would not be observed. This proved to be far better than I could ever have hoped for. The stout wooden bridge gave excellent shelter from the elements, and once I had packed some snow into where I had made my entry I was completely concealed from the world. I left a gap in the snow to allow daylight to penetrate. I was as snug as the proverbial bug in a rug. Opening the sack up I removed a cheese and one of the bottles of wine, although it might have been a brandy as it was difficult to see properly in the subdued light, but I didn't really mind which it was. Breaking off a large portion of cheese I devoured it quickly, surprised at how hungry I had become since my last rest and meal several hours earlier. Washing it down with what turned out to be wine I felt considerably better if very tired. Recalling something that my father had told me many years ago when we were out shooting pheasants in Lincolnshire I resisted the temptation to have another good swig of wine. He had told me that alcohol and wintertime are not good companions. The alcohol apparently will open up the pores in the skin and body heat will escape through sweating. Drinking might give you the impression of being warmed up, but too much under these conditions could prove fatal. With that thought I curled up for the night, determined to get as much rest and sleep before I brazenly ventured down into the village in the morning. I kept telling myself that there must be other tramps and the sort wandering about even at this time of the year. Tomorrow will tell.

The night passed very quickly and I felt refreshed and ready for the challenge that was to come. Packing my bounty away in the sack I crawled out into the open to a beautiful sunny, if chilly, morning. Climbing out of the ditch I stood for a moment on the bridge listening out. Absolute silence everywhere, a good sign. I knew I had to approach the village from the road to alleviate any suspicion from the villagers; as yet I wasn't too sure how I could achieve that. The answer was staring me in the face! I was literally standing on it. The track which ran over the bridge must lead down to the road below, why else would it be here, the villagers would need access into this forest to gather wood and tend their crops and cattle in the nearby meadows. Now was the moment then. I determinedly, although some what nervously, strode off along the track. No, that's no good, I'm walking like the service man that I am. I'm not on parade, I must slouch a little and take shorter steps, I'm a tramp not a member of His Majesties Royal Air Force and as such must behave like one. A final check of my clothing to make sure that my attire looked like those of a tramp. They would have to do.

Moving downhill now, I knew I was heading in the right direction. There, just ahead of me I could make out the clear shape of the road as it wound its way steadily to the village. This was it; there would be no going back now. Shuffling along I came nearer and nearer to my objective. I could see no signs of life, everywhere seemed totally deserted. Perhaps they were all inside their warm cottages not wanting to venture out in this weather unless they really had to. I pressed on steadily. My luck seemed to be holding. I was half way along the road and in the village proper now, but as yet no signpost that would identify this village, perhaps there would be something on the way out. Ahead of me two villagers were outside their cottage gathering in some wood from a stockpile. Looking up they both stopped to stare in my direction. I heard them clearly speak to each other and then they both roared into laughter as they continued to keep a watch on me. What should I do now? Acknowledge them or shuffle pass ignoring them. My schoolboy German would be of no use here, so I decided to look down into the snow and pay no attention to either of them, trusting to luck that they would not ask me any questions or try to engage me in conversation. I was level with them both now, about five feet away from them. Carrying on walking steadily, don't hurry, look as if I was a numbskull, these thoughts were whirring through my head. "Gutten morgen." The older looking man said. I had to respond, not to do so would only invite their curiosity and possibly more questions, leading to disaster. Slowly raising my hand I acknowledged his greeting of good morning. Moving past them the challenge that I fully expected didn't happen, instead the man who had spoke to me made some comment to his friend and again they both roared with laughter. No doubt they thought I was completely mad and had made some sarcastic remark, which they both thought was extremely funny. German humour! Moving further away now I felt relieved that I had faced the challenge and had won. Ahead of me was the one thing that had forced me to take this risk - a road sign - pointing the way to where? Stopping alongside of it as if resting for moment I glanced up at the arm. 'Obergern. 7 km.' Now I knew in which direction I was heading. As soon as it was safe to do so I would get off of this road and check my silk map, hoping that it would be marked on it, then I could set a course for Switzerland and freedom.

The opportunity presented itself just a short distance on. An open gate with a track leading up into the forest came into view. This was my chance. Looking over my shoulder to check that I had not been followed I hurried off the road and up along the track. If those two villagers could have seen me now they would have certainly been very suspicious. Quickly locating the shelter of a group of pine trees I collapsed in a heap at their base. Breathing heavily as if my lungs could not take in enough air, I felt quite dizzy and light headed. I started to shake uncontrollably, every muscle and sinew in my body rebelling against the treatment I was imposing upon it. The encounter with the two villagers really had eaten into my reserves. I resolved that I would never put myself into that situation again; from now on I would avoid people like the plague, only something so pressing that I could not justify avoiding such an encounter would persuade me from any more human contact. I recovered my breath; the shaking slowly abated and I relaxed slightly. My nerves were still on their very limits, so reaching into my sack I took out the bottles of brandy and took, against my father's advise, a long swig nearly emptying the bottle. It had the desired effect, my nerves eventually relaxed and my body stopped shaking.

Chapter 3

The Eagle's Nest

I had achieved enough for one day and realising that to press on would just invite disaster. The need for shelter until tomorrow now became my priority. The silk map and compass would have to wait until I had found a safe location to spend the rest of today and the coming night.

The sun had disappeared behind some heavy, grey clouds and the temperature became noticeably colder. Snow was on its way again. Time to move into the forest and seek refuge. Wearily struggling to my feet I moved towards a likely looking spot where the pines looked thickest. I had noticed no signs of human activity anywhere, no footprints in the snow or other indications of people were to be found, so I felt reasonably safe in the knowledge that these woods were never visited by the inhabitants of the village I had just passed through until the coming spring at the earliest. I was fortunately, totally alone here. Approaching nearer to my selected spot an old wooden shed of some description was visible just beyond. Could I be so lucky yet again? But then, I thought, why not? The villagers below would need some shelter up here to keep logging tools and farming implements to use during the summer months. With rising spirits I made my way closer, the brandy, together with lack of food, making my already unsteady progress even un-steadier! There it was, the most welcoming site that I could imagine. In front of me stood a stout, wooden shed. Groping my way to the door, I found that there was no lock on it. Standing there for a moment, I went through my 'security checks'. No unusual noises and no signs of life nearby. The snow to the door was still virginal so there had been nobody here for weeks if not months. A final look round and I pushed the door open. Once inside I closed the door shut, there being enough light filtering through a few gaps between the slats of wood panelling of the walls. My eyes slowly became accustomed to the gloom. The hut floor was of timber, so I would not, for a change, be sleeping on the damp, cold earth. A few tools were leaning against one wall, waiting until the owner came again in the spring to make use of them on his fields. There was a low partition splitting the hut into half. Making my way over for a closer investigation I was delighted to find it was full of lovely, soft hay. What a bed that would make tonight! On a shelf near the door were several interesting looking objects. Several half burnt candles, a flint striker, a saucepan, and some more smaller hand tools. Candles, together with the means to light them, and the warmth that they might give to at least, keep my hands warm. And with patience I could fill the saucepan with snow and heat this up over the candles to produce, I hoped, a warm if not boiling drink to warm me up, and with the addition of some brandy added to it would certainly help to keep the cold at bay and warm my body. Oh for some tea to go with it! This was indeed the Ritz of all of my shelters! Moving back to the door I opened it slightly, I could now see that it was snowing, not heavily, but just sufficient to cover my tracks. Feeling secure I pulled the door to and looked around at my home for the next twenty-four hours. I fully intended to rest up here for a full day and recover some strength for the days' journey that lay ahead. With ample cheese to eat and wine, which I would drink in moderation, I felt that I had sufficient rations to survive for several days, until at least, I had reached the Swiss frontier.

The time passed slowly. Outside of my sanctuary all was silence and peace, in vast contrast to the rest of the world, which was still continuing in its deadly conflict. I felt much stronger now after sleeping for most of the time curled up in the depths of the sweet smelling hay; the cheese and the energy it gave, revitalising my exhausted body, that, together with the effects of a warm brandy and water cocktail made me feel as if I could face anything that the next few weeks could throw at me, for I was absolutely certain that I would reach freedom in that time, nothing could stop me now.

I quickly but carefully gathered my few rations together and with some hesitation opened the hut's door and stepped outside to face yet more challenges. Only a sprinkling of snow had fallen to cover the evidence of my intrusion here. Making my way back to the road I had already decided that I would travel openly from now on. I turned left in the direction that would take me nearer to Switzerland and home. The town of Obergern was marked clearly on my silk map, locating my position was relatively easy once I had checked the compass bearing. So I was on my way again.

I must have walked steadily for about ten miles; it was starting to get dark now, when quite unexpectedly I came out of the forest and into a wide-open valley. The snow line was some way above me now as the path had wound through the trees on a gentle downward slope. Quickly retreating back into the trees I found a safe spot and rested up to take stock of where I found myself. I ate some cheese together with the last two squares of chocolate that I had been saving to follow. Sitting there thinking what route should I take now - should I stick to the relative safety of the forest or take a risk and go down into the valley? I looked across to the other side of the valley, where house lights lit up the early night. The day's walking had taken more out of me that I first believed. I felt mentally tired. In my confused state of mind I gave little or no thought that there would be any villages so close by. What a fool I was! I had been too confident, too clever for my own good. The cold, tension, and travelling had obviously taken its toll on me, not only physically, but also mentally. I was again becoming exhausted and this was only the third night. I estimated that I had walked probably no more than forty miles from the crash site. We were told at our evasion lectures that the Germans would throw a cordon around the crash site of some 10 - 15 miles, and if no escaping airmen were discovered then the search area would be extended to fifty miles and all towns and villages within that zone would be placed on full alert with additional security checks at railway stations and the like. Even being this far away from where I had started out I was still at great risk of being picked up. Although it was just getting dark I decided to hide up somewhere to take stock of my situation before I made a final decision, and I could do with a good rest anyway. I needed to find some shelter out of the cold or I would very probably never reach Switzerland. My earlier feelings of invincibility had been truly blown out of the window. I had been just too optimistic. Right or wrong, the decision was made! I would rest up here for a few hours and would then risk walking across the valley to where the lights offered warmth and hopefully some shelter and even food. I would have to be more vigilant and alert in my efforts to find an outbuilding or barn - with, I hoped, lovely clean, warm, welcoming straw - where I could hide out. Would the Germans think an evading airman would be so foolish and yet bold enough to try such a daring thing, to hide in the very midst of the enemy? I was hoping they wouldn't and would not search any villages for me, relying on the local population to report any strangers, and anyway, as I was probably still in their search area they had most likely thoroughly searched all of the out buildings here already.

I turned on my heels and retreated into the comparative safety of the trees where I would hide until the village would be asleep. After a few minutes a likely looking hideout appeared just off of the path on the left. A fallen pine tree, with its branches offering shelter beneath, was almost covered by drifting snow where I could burrow in and then position the broken branches to cover my way in to my new 'home'. Pushing the snow into an artificial drift, would, I hoped, be good enough to look natural and not attract any attention from either a search party or any passer by. I thought back to my previous shelter of the last two nights. This was certainly a vast difference to that, no straw to burrow into and more exposed to the elements. Never mind, I would just have to make do and be as comfortable as I could.

I made myself a rough bed from some pine twigs, curling up in a ball in an attempt to keep warm. Getting as comfortable as I could I fell into a 'half sleep', although still being acutely aware of every sound and movement around me. I lay like this for several hours until the intense cold finally woke me from my fitful sleep. It was dark now, and thick, scurrying, grey clouds moved across the face of the bright moon giving a ghostly effect to the valley and village beyond. I took out my silk escape map and miniature compass and using the light from the moon I calculated that I was somewhere in the mountains above Salzburg, an area of Southern Germany close to the Austrian border. Squatting on the cold damp earth I ate the last piece of cheese. Delving deeper into the sack I pulled out the last bottle and all that remained of the wine, removing the cork for the last time l took several big gulps until that too, was all consumed. Discarding the now empty and useless sack I sat there for a moment, deep in thought. Why didn't I stay in the woodman's hut where it had been safer and a great deal more comfortable? I could have foraged for food and hid there until the weather improved. Instead I find myself here in a poor shelter and with no food or water. If I couldn't find both I seriously doubted if I could continue. Would a prisoner of war camp be so bad? At least I would be fed and sheltered, and amongst friends. A terrible depression suddenly descended upon me. "Come on! Snap out of it." I shouted to myself. This is just what we were warned about. 'Think positive,' we had been told. If you couldn't then you would be finished. I closed my eyes to shut out these negative thoughts. There, in my mind's eye, I saw them again. My crew mates, my good friends. There they were, encouraging me not to give up, but to press on. I opened my eyes to find that the skies had cleared and the moon was now shining brightly ready to guide me onward. A sign from God indeed. I would not give up now! With that positive thought in my mind I gathered the remains of my escape kit together and left my hideout and retraced my steps along the path. Cautiously crossing over a narrow paved road that I was not really expecting, a dirt road would have been more appropriate for this backwoods part of the Third Reich. I stealthily moved towards the ever beckoning village lights. Moving as quickly as I could across the open fields I was relieved to discover that there was very little snow in which to leave any evidence of my presence.

Eventually reaching the outskirts of the village I hid behind a low wooden fence to the side of one of the houses. From this vantage point I could see that the village had a wide main street with one or two minor streets leading off from it. The main road and pavements were surprisingly clear of all snow, as if it had been swept. Streetlights were glowing brightly at each end of the village and one or two others were on either side of the road giving partial illumination along its length. Every light had a swastika flag hanging from it, swaying slightly in the light evening breeze.

There were about twenty or thirty houses constructed in typical Bavarian manner on each side of the road. Some had whitewashed walls, others were plain, clearly showing the red brick construction, all had exposed wooden beams and red tiled roofs and as I would fully have expected hanging from the windows and roof gutters, were swastika flags. Moving slightly I looked along the road where I could make out a small hotel or Inn at the far end near to what appeared to be a military barracks, clearly illuminated by several lights. There were, unexpectedly, two anti-aircraft batteries positioned to either side of the barracks. This I found rather puzzling. This was not an area of any strategic importance worth attacking by Bomber Command that I was aware of. There were no industrial targets here to defend so why the need for these anti-aircraft guns?

Curiosity got the better of me. Leaving my cover I decided to move down the street, dodging from shadow to shadow to get closer and to take a better look. Luckily for me there wasn't a soul to be seen anywhere, the local population were either tucked up all snug and warm inside their houses, or taking a social drink with their neighbours at the Inn, where I prayed, they would stay while I was investigating. Wild ideas began to spring up in my mind; could this be a secret location for Hitler's so called super weapons we had heard about - if they actually existed at all that is? No, surely they wouldn't be located in a civilian area. If there was anything of any bombing value here, then it was my duty to find out and report it when I eventually returned to England.

Moving quietly and stealthily, I moved further into the town. Using every possible hiding place to make my way along the deserted streets I managed to get as near as I dare to the barracks. Judging from the size of the building and number of widows it was large enough to accommodate perhaps no more than a hundred soldiers. Alongside of the swastika draped in front of the building another flag was also hanging in prominence. This I instantly recognised with some trepidation. It was that of the dreaded and much feared SS, Himmler's uniformed band of thugs and murderers, often referred to as Himmler's private army, and very much a law unto themselves.

The barracks was not manned by soldiers of the Wermacht as I first thought, but by troops of Himmler's elite own force of crack soldiers, their allegiance sworn to Adolf Hitler, Heinrich Himmler, the Nazi Party and the Third Reich, serving Hitler and the Nazi Party until death, feared more than the Gestapo for their brutality. What was so important here in this small, peaceful looking Bavarian village to warrant such a large presence?

I felt sure that the answer lay along the road leading out of the village and further up into the tree-lined slopes past these barracks. I came across a signpost with the village name on it - Berchtesgaden.

I moved even more cautiously now, bypassing the barracks by taking a circular route down a grassy slope and around to the other side eventually regaining the road. Looking back towards the barracks I could clearly see by the light of one of the streetlights that there was a stout barrier across the road with a sentry box alongside of it. I could not see any signs of a sentry, but was sure that it must have been manned.

Grateful for the semi darkness that hid me from any alert eyes looking my way I turned around and quietly headed off along this mysterious road. The pale moonlight helped me to navigate my way along this well constructed road that passed through several short tunnels as it wound for some distance alongside open grassland. At the end of a valley on the left I noticed an area of cleared pasture that could easily have been used as an airstrip for light aircraft. I knew that it was far too small to accommodate anything bigger; our runway back in Lincolnshire was several thousand feet long, this grass strip was nowhere near that length. There was definitely the outline of a grass runway with a small hanger like structure to one side. I could also make out a road leading down to it, from, I assumed, the very road I was now walking along. I continued upwards, more determined than ever to find some answers.

Above me through the pine trees, which seemed to cling precariously to the mountainside, I noticed a number of what appeared to be house lights clearly shining through the branches. Moving forward cautiously now I could make out the outline of a very grand looking building, more like a villa, standing out in the moonlight. Could this be the reason the SS troops were stationed in the village below? I certainly hadn't come across anything else that might have warranted their presence here. I felt that the answers to all my questions would soon become apparent.

I moved along the road, on and ever upwards towards the villa that was now clearly visible in the moonlight high up in an open clearing above the trees. I was being drawn to its shining lights, attracting me very much in the same way in which a moth is drawn to a flickering candle, but not, I prayed silently to God, to the same fate when the moth is eventually consumed within the flames. I knew deep down that it was a foolhardy thing for me to carry on, and that if I had been in a different frame of mind and not almost at the point of mental and physical exhaustion I would have taken a more wiser decision which would have taken me away from here and nearer my real goal of reaching Switzerland. But I carried on. There was no going back now, I had come this far without being detected and would push Lady Luck to the limits.

Moving forward once again I became very conscious of the sound of crunching gravel underfoot. I stopped in my tracks. The sound must have carried quite clearly in the cold night air and must have surely been heard? I stood quite still, listening intently for any possible activity from ahead or behind in response to the noise I had made, but all seemed quiet. The only sound I could hear was the panting of my own heavily laboured breathing. I noticed that there was a grass bank running along on each side of the road, and without further hesitation I moved off of the road and carried on walking on the grass.

The road wound its way up and up ever higher into the wooded slopes, passing through several more short tunnels cut out of the solid rock of the mountainside. I must have already had walked steadily now for well over an hour. At last I came round a slight bend in the road and the villa stood out in front of me. I rested against one of its walls to regain my breath before continuing. Standing there listening to my heart beating loudly within my chest I was staggered to discover, that although it was extremely cold, I was sweating sufficiently to soak my uniform right through to the lining of the old greatcoat.

Having regained my breath I stepped forwards very carefully, I peered around the corner of the wall, my hands feeling its cold rough surface as I did so. A long flight of broad, stone or granite steps, lead up to what appeared to be an extensive paved terraced area. Standing there quietly for a moment, I listened intently to see if my approach had been discovered. All appeared to be quiet, so I decided to continue up the steps, fearing at any moment to be challenged by whoever lived here. Keeping against the side of the wall and remaining in the shadows, I eventually reached the top of the steps, where, as I first thought, they opened onto a very substantial terrace. Here and there were placed various chairs and recliners together with several tables with folded umbrellas. From the light of the moon I could see that on the far side of the terrace there were magnificent views of the surrounding mountains, the moonlight reflecting from the snow on their crests. To my right was a long open veranda that ran the whole length of the villa and had several open archways leading out onto the terrace. This was no local Burgomaster's villa or that of some minor Nazi Party leader. It was plainly obvious from what little I could see that a great deal of time and planning, let alone money, had gone into constructing this magnificent building.

A slight wind disturbed the still night air. From above me the movement of something fluttering in the breeze caught my eyes. Looking up I saw several flags with the Nazi swastika emblem on them. That should have started warning bells ringing in my head, but I was just too exhausted after my journey here to realise at this moment what I had stumbled into. My mind was a jumble of different thoughts. I must have time to think! I was even more confused now, and stumbling upon this building with these Nazi emblems everywhere had possibly only made my escape to Switzerland a lot more difficult if not impossible. I was yet to realise just how difficult it was to become.

I couldn't possibly hide up here, there was no suitable place to conceal myself through the day ahead, plus there would undoubtably be many people moving around the villa. Guards, probably with dogs, would no doubt be regularly patrolling the area. I needed time to think. Returning to my hiding place was the only and best option. I turned around and as silently as I had first approached the villa, retraced my footsteps back the way I had came and headed back along the road to the village and my hiding place to decide what to do next. All this had taken many hours and I had lost all track of time in my excitement and determination to discover just what was going on here. It was now fast approaching dawn, so I was forced to run down the road stumbling in places in my haste, this was the same road that just a few minutes earlier I had so very casually strolled along!

Stumbling along I finally came near to the barrier across the road stopping some distance from it. Again there was no sign of a sentry on duty, although I was sure that there had to be. Leaving the road by way of the grass bank I headed in the general direction of where I believed my shelter to be. I ran across the meadow as fast as my weary legs could carry me, trying to spot any familiar landmarks as I went.

In front of me was a gap in the trees where I knew I had first stepped out of the forest and into the meadow. I altered my course, making my way towards it as quickly as I could. Finally reaching it I desperately headed for my shelter. Gasping for breath I collapsed in a tangled heap of arms and legs behind the branches and snow drifts where I had rested just a few hours ago. Had I been observed? There were no shouts of alarm that I could hear, surely if I had been seen all hell would have been let loose by now. The rising sun was just poking its fiery head over the roofs of the houses, so I had to secure my hiding place quickly from any prying eyes. I pushed more snow up into my entranceway to block it off completely from the outside world. Totally exhausted I collapsed onto the ground, fighting for breath, every muscle in my body screaming out in rebellion for the way I had forced it into going on. Feeling more secure now that I was safely hidden I had to think everything over and decide on my next move.

Through a hazy mist inside my head I attempted to make sense of everything. The villa was festooned in Nazi regalia and was obviously of some importance. Perhaps it belonged to the local Burgomaster - no, it was far too grand for that. Possibly some high-ranking Nazi official? I wasn't convinced by that theory either. That might explain the presence of regular German army troops, but not the SS. Perhaps a member of Hitler's governing body? Could Heinrich Himmler, head of the SS, be living here? That was a definite possibility. The more I struggled for answers, the more confused I became. This was no good at all. I was getting angry with myself. What to do now? Should I try and skirt around it and push on to Switzerland and safety or investigate further? If it was of some military importance I should at least attempt to discover as much as I could, so that when, and if, I finally managed to return to England, I could pass on what may turn out to be some very valuable information to our military and security services. I was so totally confused now.

Pangs of hunger were tormenting my stomach. Searching through the deep pockets of my greatcoat I frantically felt for any food that I might have put there and forgotten about. With a sigh of relief my fingers found in one pocket the last of the chocolate and some Horlicks tablets that had been there since I found the cheeses. In the other pocket the remains of a half eaten turnip, not a great feast but enough to satisfy the cravings I felt in my rumbling stomach. I would have given a year's wages for a strong, sweet cup of tea and bacon and eggs right now! I would rest and try to get some sleep and decide what would be the best course of action when I woke up, but I already knew in my mind that I had to investigate more - regardless of what risk it posed. So I settled down, curling up into a ball, covering myself with the old greatcoat to keep as warm as I could. Exhaustion finally overtook me and I drifted off into a deep, if troubled, sleep.

The intense cold woke me up. I had slept far better than I thought I would and felt surprisingly refreshed. So, what to do now? I had decided that I would return to the villa and try to discover as much as I could, and who knows, if I was really lucky perhaps I could find some food. But should I first destroy the insignia on my uniform and get rid of any sort of identification just in case I was caught? I wouldn't want to give too much easy information to the enemy. No, I would leave them. I could then at least prove to be a shot down RAF flyer and be accorded the protection of the Geneva Convention.

Darkness was now rapidly approaching. I could see a full moon high up in the darkening sky and believed at first that it would assist me in my task, but it could also work against me. Any one looking out from one of the many windows in the village would easily spot me crossing the valley and coming up along the road. I had to accept the risk, after all, I had succeeded last night, and with Lady Luck still on my side I should be safe enough. I would have to be extra alert, and although I felt quite weak after what I had endured over the last few days, I made up my mind that anyone getting in my way would wish that they hadn't!

I retraced my steps back to the road. Walking as quietly as I could I stopped every few minutes to make sure I had not been observed - I assumed that if I had been spotted, a right royal 'hue and cry' would happen, but as long as everything remained quiet I was pretty sure I was safe. Eventually I managed to make my way safely back to the base of the steps that led up to the terrace without incident.

Stopping for a few moments in the shadows I listened intently for any sign of a sentry who might be patrolling the grounds. I didn't encounter such a sentry last night, but that didn't mean that one wouldn't be on duty now. The only sound I could hear was that of my heart beating loudly as if it would explode at any moment.

Having satisfied myself that the coast was, as far as I could tell, all clear, I stepped away from the wall placing one foot on the bottom step. What was that? Was that a slight movement? Was a man standing quite still in the shadows? I instantly froze, not daring to move. But I couldn't just stand here and hope I wouldn't be spotted so I edged myself very slowly back into the protection of the welcome shadows. He must have either been dozing or believing that nobody would come uninvited at this late hour was not as alert as he should have been, probably relying on the sentry at the barrier below to alert him to any visitors arriving by car by a telephone call. Either way I had been very lucky and thanked Lady Lucky again. How I even managed to reach the top of terrace on my earlier 'visit' without being detected I will never know, perhaps my luck was getting better! I obviously couldn't attempt to go ahead up the wide flight of steps now, he would surely challenge me and that would be that! What to do? I noticed that there was an earth bank that dropped sharply away from the road directly opposite the steps. If I could reach the bank without being seen I could make my way along it and beneath road level out of sight and in the shadows to get to a position somewhere behind him. I had to make the attempt, there was no other way of reaching the terrace and eventually the interior of the villa without climbing the steps, and to do that this guard had to go!

Taking advantage of a fleeting cloud scurrying across the face of the moon I quickly and silently moved to the other side of the road and carefully slid down the side of the bank. I lay there perfectly still for a moment. No movement or shout of a challenge came from the guard. Being in Germany he obviously thought that there would be no possibility of an intruder being anywhere close by. If only he knew! The placing of this man was most likely just a token gesture on the orders of whoever lived here.

I could see him quite clearly now, his dark uniform standing out in silhouette against the lighter moon lit colour of the terrace. I slowly edged my way towards him, slowly, so very slowly. My body was as tense as a violin string, but somehow - perhaps it was the adrenaline pumping through my veins - I managed to get to a position just a few yards behind his post. I realised that I would only have the one attempt at disabling him, but how? I was not really strong enough to fight him man to man, and the noise of any scuffle would most likely alert any other sentries who may be posted elsewhere. Suddenly, an idea! I removed one of my bootlaces. It was at least four foot long and made of a very strong and thick cord. This would be ideal to strangle him as long as I could just get close enough without being detected. If I couldn't all would be lost. At best a quick end from a bullet would be the result.

Binding the ends of the cord around each hand in readiness to loop over his head and around his neck I crept forward not daring to even breath. Nearer and nearer I crept until I could hear his breath in the cold night air. If he should turn round now all would be lost! Leaping forward the last couple of feet I looped the cord over his helmet, around his thick bull like neck and pulled the cord tight with all of my remaining strength. Instinctively he tried to grasp the cord with his hands, but I was too quick, the cord tightening around his throat as I choked the very life out of him. It was a brief struggle, I had caught him completely by surprise, and he slumped slowly to the ground, his arms and hands now dangling uselessly at his sides. It was done! My whole body was shaking violently as I also collapsed to the ground along side his now still body.

I had never been this close to the enemy before, let alone kill one hand to hand. To smell his body odour and feel the heat of his body made me feel quite sick for a moment. I had killed my first enemy and was quite repulsed by it. But why should I feel like that? He would have had no hesitation in killing me, after all, that is what he was trained to do. That was the difference between us. I did my killing from 20.000 feet; he did his face to face. He could see his enemy, I couldn't.

I had to dispose of him. Recovering my senses I quickly removed his pistol - I felt a lot better with some type of weapon in my hand - and dragged him and his rifle silently behind his post into the shrubbery. I searched his body for anything that could be of use to me, and finding nothing, rolled his body down the earth bank and into the shadows at the bottom. Hastily replacing my bootlace I ventured out of the shadows and again made my way up the wide flight of stone steps whilst hugging the side of the wall to use the cover of any shadows or niches.

The terrace was partly illuminated from several lights shining through a series of windows on the second floor above me and on my right. Moving forward past the vaulted open veranda I came to a corner of the villa. Turning the corner I was amazed to discover a huge window that virtually replaced the whole lower ground floor wall. Backing away into the shadows I took stock of my position. Looking around onto the terrace I could clearly make out the terrace furniture that was scattered about. The moonlight seemed to reflect off of the mountain slopes opposite as if to encourage me to go on. I checked the safety catch was in the 'off' position on the pistol for I fully intended to use it if the situation arose, although I wasn't thinking about any consequences of what any aggression on my part would bring. Discovering what this villa was used for and who lived here was my main concern, and then to get whatever information I had back to England via Switzerland. I must therefore be as cautious and as patient as a wildcat hunting down his prey.

There appeared to be no more guards anywhere. My luck was still with me. I became braver now, or was it still the adrenaline coursing through my body? Either way, I left the sanctuary of the wall and shadows and stepped a single pace into the open, on the alert and ready to use my pistol. No alarms sounded, no shouting of being discovered, absolute silence and peace. Bolstered by this I moved further out onto the terrace. I had to take care, there were low tables and seats scattered everywhere, the last thing I needed was to fall over one of these. I could have done with another friendly cloud now; it really was bright up here away from the trees of the forest below and on the other side of the valley.

There was a solid, wooden panelled door just in front of me, so moving swiftly and silently I made my way to it. I took hold of its ornate metal handle and carefully and silently turned it. The door opened easily and silently thankfully, but then I thought, why should it be locked? I was in the very heart of the Third Reich, where else would the villa's owner feel so secure? With shaking hands I very cautiously pushed the door open slightly. Hearing no challenge from within I took a deep breath and boldly opened it fully. With the pistol ready in my hand I stepped inside, closing the door quietly behind me. Adjusting my eyes to the bright electric lights I could see that this room was furnished with chairs and tables made of what appeared to be a white plaited cane. A tall metal standard lamp that had been left switched on stood against the far wall. There were a couple of tropical plants in large pots opposite a low wooden cupboard that had a curious display of cacti plants on it. I say curious because this is the last place I would have expected to find plants that are more accustomed to warmer climates. The floor was carpeted almost from wall to wall. Polished wooden floor timbers were exposed along the four sides of the carpet. Two leaded windows, the full width and height of the room, looked out onto the terrace and to the mountains in the distance. With such a magnificent view as this I could now understand why the villa had been built here. Total seclusion virtually atop of the mountain which stood dominating the village and meadows far below.

As silently as I could and with the pistol still at the ready, I moved on through this room to another door at the far end. Standing there for a moment I listened carefully for any movement or sound of voices from the other side, nothing, all was quiet. I opened this door to discover that it led into a corridor that had several more doors to either side. Still no sign of any activity from within, so I crept forward to investigate a door which was slightly ajar. Again listening for any noise to indicate that this room might be occupied I pushed the door open and entered. What an amazing room this turned out to be. Beautiful ornate pine panelling decorated every wall from floor to ceiling; a very impressive solid oak desk stood at one end of the room; behind the desk stood a high backed carved wood and leather-covered chair. At the other end stood four chairs and a settee. These were designed for comfort and all had richly coloured fabric covering them, each had several deep cushions where the occupant could settle down in comfort and ease. Standing in between the four chairs was a very ornate carved oak coffee table with a few document papers spread about on it. The light emitted from a small lamp on the coffee table and several wall lights was enough for me to see the room clearly. I noticed there were several framed photographs on the coffee table, moving across to it I couldn't resist picking one up. It held a photograph of a man in military uniform and a very attractive woman. I couldn't quite make out who the man was, but I assumed he was the owner of this magnificent villa and was obviously some high ranking party official to have such a fine place. Putting it carefully back in the same spot I moved on. On the walls were several watercolour sketches that could have been painted by the villa's owner as they gave the appearance of a very amateur hand. Luckily the floor was carpeted the same as the other room which helped me to move silently about.I couldn't really believe my good luck. Here I was blatantly walking through this very grand villa and nobody was here to challenge me! Leaving this room I went out into the corridor once again and into another room further on. This was a magnificent bedroom. This time two bedside lights had been left on. The colour scheme was a distinct light jade colour, as was the corridor. It looked as if the walls were decorated with very old engravings to match what appeared to be antique furniture. The differences in decor in the rooms I had dared to inspect was quite surprising - from cacti and other sub-tropical plants to engravings and antiques.

I had seen enough. There was nothing in here that could help me establish who lived here. Now was the time to get out before my luck ran out and I was discovered. I slowly made my way back the same way I had entered leaving every thing exactly as I had found it. Back on the terrace once again I made my way silently in the shadows to the other side of the villa in the hope of discovering more information.

Suddenly raised voices! I stopped dead in my tracks as if I had become suddenly frozen to the spot. I quickly recovered my wits and spun around to look behind me, gun in hand and ready to fire. Nobody was there, so where had the voices come from and had I been spotted? Again there was shouting but this time I could tell that it was not aimed at me. No, they were not raised as if in alarm, more like arguing. The voices were coming through windows from a room several feet in front of me. If I had been a few steps further on I could well have been passing this very window and been spotted. I moved silently to the corner of the window, and, carefully peering between a tall potted plant of some description, I could see quite clearly into the room where the raised voices came from.

In the middle of this richly furnished room was a huge carved wooden desk covered in what appeared to be maps and other documents. The largest of the maps had pointers and miniature flags on sticks placed at various positions. There was one very ornately carved, heavy wooden chair at the desk, with a high solid back so it was impossible for me to see who was sitting there. Opposite were one or two more chairs, but from my position it was difficult to see clearly. I could just make out a uniformed man, standing with his hunched back to me as he lent over the table examining the maps or whatever they were. He was undoubtedly the owner of this villa and who was obviously of some importance. On the opposite side of the desk stood a very smartly dressed German Wehrmacht officer. This officer I noticed, had thick red stripes running down the side of his uniform trousers and he was highly decorated. I recognised at least one of his many decorations, it was the Nights Cross, one of Germany's highest military awards. He was obviously a 'soldier's soldier' as he had apparently had some injury to his left arm as it was heavily bandaged and in a sling inside his uniform jacket, the sleeve being pinned to the jacket lapel. I wondered if the Iron Cross had only recently been awarded to him because of this injury possibly sustained in a recent battle?

The man hunched over the desk was speaking now. I could just make out what he was saying - my German language lessons at school would be worthwhile after all! The Russians were mentioned, and Stalin in particular. 'Barbarossa'. What did that mean? The officer appeared to be in total disagreement with what the other man was saying, he stood there shaking his head in disagreement and indicating to other areas of the map, moving the marker flags as he did so. I could sense, that, watching and listening through the window, this high-ranking officer was losing the argument, to who, I assumed, must be his obvious superior.

The seated man suddenly leapt up, banging the desk heavily several times in a vicious temper, he sent the maps and flags flying across the desk and onto the floor, shouting and shaking his fists at the other man. He was in such a rage that his whole body was shaking uncontrollably. The high-ranking officer immediately snapped to attention. Looking shaken and ashen faced he gave the Nazi salute and smartly turning on his heels he walked from the room closing the two heavy wooden doors as he went. This was an officer of some importance and yet he had been obviously over-ruled in no uncertain terms and had been instantly dismissed.

I moved back into the shadows. I had to take stock of all this. Going over in my head all that I had observed I struggled to find an answer. I was still trying to find that answer when the man rose from the desk and turned towards the window. At last I could see his features quite clearly. My eyes seemed to pop out of my head and my jaw certainly dropped in utter disbelief and shock. There was now no doubt as to who he was. I recognised him immediately. That short comical moustache which had been so cleverly characterised in so many English newspapers, magazines and films, left no doubt in my mind. Adolf Hitler! If I could have reached out through the thick glass that kept us apart I could easily have touched him. The most hated man in the whole of Europe was standing just a few feet from me.

If I could just get the information back to Bomber Command about this place they could blast it off the face of the Earth. But what if I didn't make it back? What then? Whether from the cold or mental and physical tiredness I wasn't sure, but a crazy voice spoke to me very loudly from within my head. I had the means within my grasp to strike the blow that would surely end this terrible war. Kill Hitler! I looked slowly down at the pistol in my now shaking hand. I had the means and I had been chosen by fate to be the appointed executioner. I could end this terrible war if only I had the courage. The voice kept on urging me on; it was the only thought inside my head now. Somehow I knew that I had to kill Hitler.

But how could I get into the room to confront and shoot this madman who had turned Europe into a continent of death, destruction, and utter misery? The noise of furniture being violently moved rang out from inside. Shouting in rage, Hitler had pushed the heavy chair to one side and swept away from the desktop the remaining documents that hadn't been flung to the floor in his earlier outburst. Standing there for a moment in silence, he turned around and began to walk over towards the windows where I was hiding. Shrinking further into the shadows now, not daring to move, I watched as he came ever closer. He was standing in front of the window, looking out across the terrace to the distant mountains, his face distorted in anger. Stepping to one side he raised his hand and appeared to press or turn on a switch. Electric motors started whirring and incredibly the window was slowly sliding down into a cavity within the walls and floor. This was an amazing stroke of luck. I had heard senior officers say that winning a battle is 90% luck and 10% planning and this was one of those occasions that proved just how true that was! The window was now almost out of sight, steadily lowering into the floor cavity.

With the window finally vanishing into the depths he strode onto the terrace, his footsteps echoing clearly throughout the cold night air. Stopping briefly, taking in a deep breath of the clean night air, he passed by me within inches of where I was concealed. He was slowly and purposely making his way to the low wall that surrounded the terrace, his hands clenched behind his back in suppressed rage and occasionally exaggerating his rage by stamping heavily onto the patio paving and uttering curses. Stopping at the low stone built wall he stood gazing at the image of the far off mountains, his hands resting on top of the wall. The moment seemed very surreal. It was so peaceful here looking at the snow on the peaks shining brightly in the moonlight, in stark contrast to what this man was responsible for in Europe, the death and destruction he had unleashed. This was the moment I had silently been praying for; it was to be now or never.

I stepped out of the shadows and advanced quietly towards him, my every footstep seemed to echo loudly although in truth I knew that they were hardly audible. He must hear me surely I thought to myself. After what seemed an eternity Hitler's back was now just a few inches away from me. Slowly but deliberately raising the pistol in my shaking hands I took aim at the back of his head - and fired! One, two, three shots in rapid succession at point blank range found their way straight into Hitler's skull which violently exploded into a thousand bloody fragments of bone and flesh, some splattering my face and upper body. The force of the bullets propelled him forward onto the low wall where he fell and slumped in a grotesque death throw on top of it. His blood poured onto the stone slabs of the terrace, leaving a pool of bright red blood which slowly spread and mixed in with the light layer of snow turning it a deep shade of crimson, clearly visible in the moonlight. Adolf Hitler was dead and I had killed him! Feeling violently sick I almost collapsed on top of his lifeless body, but calling on my last reserves of innermost strength managed to steady myself.

Swaying from side to side my hands slowly dropped to my sides, both of them shaking violently, the pistol still gripped tightly in my right hand, my finger still around the trigger. I had not given any thought of what to do next, everything thing had happened so quickly. This felt so unreal - like existing in a foggy dream, but this was no dream. I wanted to kill Adolf Hitler, and I had succeeded. My head started to clear; the shooting would surely bring guards rushing out to discover the cause.

I could hear the heavy boots of men racing up the steps, their steel heel plates echoing loudly, coming ever closer, now they were on the terrace speeding towards me, doors were being flung open wide, the sound of men shouting and calling to each other announcing their arrival. Floodlights, switched on from within the villa, now brightly illuminated the terrace. I could not escape; there was nowhere to escape to. A bullet in my own brain crossed my mind, which would be far better than capture, torture and then the execution squad. I somehow managed to raise my still shaking hands up to my head with the full intent of ending my life. Squeezing the trigger nothing happened, I tried again, nothing. The chamber was empty. There had only been those three rounds in it. Now shock came over me. I suddenly felt very light headed, a swirling mist appeared in front of my eyes and the mountains started to spin ever faster. I collapsed onto the ground alongside Hitler's body in a dead feint, a heavy dark grey mist blotting out my vision as I passed into a world in limbo, not being fully conscious in the real world and yet not quite into the dark world that beckoned me to enter.

Slowly the mist began to clear. I was no longer outside on the terrace, but inside the villa. It was all now beginning to come back to me. It was probably only the intervention of a high ranking officer, most likely to be the same one I had seen with Hitler, that had prevented me from being beaten to death where I lay alongside the body of Hitler. I can now remember the searing pain of being brutally kicked by, I assume, members of his SS bodyguard. Almost at the point of passing out I heard an order instructing them to stop and to bring me inside the villa. Two burly soldiers grabbed hold of my ankles and dragged me by my feet across the stone terrace and through the same entrance that Hitler had walked passed me just a few minutes ago.

The two soldiers picked me up from the floor and very roughly sat me in the very same chair that Hitler had recently occupied, which I thought, was quite ironic.

The officer ordered the guards to stand to one side, and standing in front of me addressed me in German. My fog enshrouded brain couldn't comprehend what he was saying, so I replied in English, just giving him my name, rank and serial number, repeating it several times. The silence and atmosphere in the room that followed my wavering voice was electrifying.

"You are an Englander?" It was the officer speaking again. I could tell from the tone in his voice that my disclosure of my identity came as a complete and utter surprise to him. Silence again followed. He stared at me in bewilderment and complete disbelief. Recovering, he spoke loudly to the guards issuing orders. I couldn't understand what had been said. Turning smartly on his heels, he spun around and I heard him walk away and leave the room. The guards came over to me, another beating I thought, but no, they remained at attention to either side of me obviously to make sure that I wasn't going to attempt to escape, they could have saved their selves the effort though, I was in no state to get up from the chair, let alone to try and make a break for freedom!

The officer returned after what seemed to be several hours. More gruff commands and I was manhandled out of the villa, but not before my hands were handcuffed behind my back. Half walking and half being dragged, I was taken down the same steps that a few hours ago had led me to the terrace. Waiting at the bottom was a black limousine with the back door already open. I was bundled inside, a guard on either side of me, one of whom held a Luger pistol at the ready. The officer sat in the front with the driver and with a motorcycle escort we sped off into the night.

It was a short drive direct to the SS barracks at Berchtesgaden where I was held in a well guarded cell until I assumed, arrangements could be made for me to be questioned by expert interrogators, meaning the Gestapo. Surprisingly I was given medical attention and some food and drink, no doubt to make sure that I could live long enough to tell the Gestapo all that they wanted to know. But after that what would be my fate? Surely now that Adolf Hitler was dead the whole course of the war would be changed. Would the new leaders of the Third Reich attempt to reach a peace settlement with the Allies to end the destruction that Hitler had unleashed upon the world. If that was the case then it is just possible that I could survive after all and be returned to England eventually. Only time would tell.

Another black limousine and two Gestapo officers, wearing their trade mark black leather overcoats and trilby hats arrived later that night. My cell door was unlocked and I was instructed by one of the Gestapo men, in excellent English, to follow him out to the waiting car. A short ride to an airfield that must have been the same one I had spotted on my way up to the villa, where I boarded the Junkers transport aircraft that was waiting there, its engines running, ready for take off. Down the grass runway and then up into the lightening sky as dawn rapidly approached with a new day and whatever it was to hold in store for me. There then followed a short flight to what I recognised from the aircraft window as Berlin, after all, I had bombed it more than once at night and could easily make out the bomb damage which Allied bombers had inflicted upon the very heart of the Third Reich. I also realised that Berlin is where the Gestapo had their headquarters.

As a Royal Air Force crewmember I knew that the Luftwaffe should have interrogated me, but obviously they had been by-passed and the Gestapo were to be trusted with the task of my interrogation. The Junkers touched down smoothly and as it came to a halt I was quickly ushered off into a waiting car that had pulled up alongside of the aircraft even before the pilot had cut his engines. Not a word was spoken either to me or between my escorts. My only 'contact' with them was either a nudge or a push in my back indicating where I should go and what I was expected to do.

We drove quickly through Berlin, along streets that in places, were still being cleared of rubble from an earlier, probably last night, bombing raid. Tonight would be no different! If only the Royal Air Force and Bomber Command knew that they would be dropping their bombs onto me! We stopped outside a very impressive building on the Prinz Albrecht Strasse, the very heart of the Gestapo. This is where I was to be interrogated.

Needing no invitation from anybody, I stepped out of the car; again my escorts spoke no words. I was pushed and jostled up the flight of steps leading to the main doors, once through I was half carried, half dragged along winding corridors to a cell deep within the heart of the building and bundled into a cell to await my fate. There were no witnesses as to my arrival, the marble reception desk and foyer were deserted, as if nobody was to know who I was or that I was even in the building. The cell door was slammed shut, a bolt noisily slid into place, a key turned, and I was alone. Seeing a bed and mattress in one corner I staggered over to it, my ribs still in pain from the beating I had been given. With great relief to my aching body I lay down to await my fate whatever it might be. Lady Luck had deserted me now;

I really was on my own. High up in one of the walls was a small barred window, just too high to be able to look out of but allowing just a small glimmer of daylight to enter the cell. A single light bulb hanging from an old flex in the ceiling gave enough illumination for me to make out that the only furniture in the cell apart from the wooden bed alongside one wall with its filthy mattress and a single threadbare cover was a metal bucket in the corner, which I assumed, were the toilet facilities.

So this was it then, the start of what I knew would be a very unpleasant experience. Would my life end here? What torture would these people inflict on me, and could I endure it? I decided then and there that I would tell them whatever they wanted to know apart from anything that could put my fellow squadron members at risk. My name, rank and serial number, being shot down and the crash and subsequent events leading up to my assassination of Adolf Hitler would be the only other details to pass my lips. They would either believe me or not. I had no doubt that I would end up facing a firing squad, unless of course, the new German leaders sued for peace and I would, by some miracle, manage to survive and eventually be repatriated to England. Only time would tell, and I prayed that time would be on my side.

Chapter 4

Imprisonment & Interrogation

I woke up in the now dark cell. Dazed, I attempted to sit up but couldn't move. I could feel the cold metal of the cuffs and manacles that were locked securely and tightly onto my wrists and ankles making sure that I couldn't escape. How long had I been unconscious? I had no idea how much time had passed. Had I been in a crazy dream and was I still in it? My memory started to return as my head slowly cleared. I wondered if I had been given some sort of drug to keep me subdued. It was all very slowly coming back to me now. The blazing Lancaster, crashing to the earth below, managing to bail out some how, the landing in the forest and attempting to reach Switzerland, and knowing that my crew were all dead. The realisation of what had passed suddenly dawned on me, hitting me like a ten-ton army truck. I really had shot Hitler and this was not the mad dream of some maniac. Suddenly vivid images began to flash before my eyes. I could see again the pistol in my shaking hands, raising it up to Hitler's head and then pulling the trigger three times. Raising it again to my own head and pulling the trigger but to no avail, the chamber was empty. I remember passing out, but after that nothing, a complete blank, until a few moments ago when I came to here. I lay here quietly for a moment trying desperately to get my mind and brain working properly again. It was no use, I was too exhausted, I lay down on the filthy smelling straw filled mattress; my eyelids were too heavy for me to stop them from closing over my eyes. Fighting a loosing battle with them my eyes slowly closed and sleep overcame me instantly. What would tomorrow bring?

I had no idea how long I had been asleep, was it just minutes or several hours? I had no way of knowing, time was lost in this place of despair and misery. The bolt and lock on the door were noisily unlocked and the cell door was flung open, banging loudly against the wall. Standing there were two SS prison guards, each holding a wicked looking truncheon, ready no doubt, to be used at the slightest excuse; a few short steps into the cell and both were standing menacingly at my side. One of them shouted a command at me, needing no second bidding I attempted to get up from the bed, obviously I was not quick enough as a sharp, sickening blow to my shoulders knocked me back down. Amid more shouting two hands grasped my arms and hauled me up where, for a moment, I wavered from side to side as I tried to get my balance. A punch into my kidneys and I doubled up in agony. "Raus, raus." The guards were screaming at me. I hobbled over to the door as best I could and was pushed into the direction these two brutes wanted me to take. Ahead were some steps leading down into the lower depths, I felt as if I was descending into Hell as I was 'encouraged' to go down them. They led into a single room illuminated with a single light hanging from the ceiling. In the gloom I could make out two more guards standing each side of a solitary chair, but these two were different, they were stripped from the waist up, their bodies glistening with sweat. Forced to sit down, my hands were roughly manacled behind my back by one of them. The other grabbed hold of my hair and pulled my face up high. I had no illusions why I was here - torture to make me speak and possibly death at their barbaric hands.

A strong light shining directly into my face blinded me. I closed my eyes and moved my head to one side in an effort to avoid its intense brightness; it was so bright it hurt my eyes to look at it. A hand took hold of my head and twisted it directly towards it, fingers then forced my eyelids open, and at the same time tape was applied to them preventing me from closing my eyes. Question followed question, relentlessly these two sadists fired questions at me giving me no time to think. I kept telling them that I was a shot down British bomber pilot but to no avail. The light was extinguished and I was hoisted from the old wooden chair and dragged over to what appeared to be a bathtub. A sharp kick into to back of my knees and I was down on the cold stone floor as if kneeling in prayer.

Hands took hold of my shoulders and my head was forced into the freezing cold water in the bath. They held me here for just long enough before pulling my head out at the moment when I would surely drown. More questions in perfect English - "What was your mission in Germany?" "What is your code name?" "Who is your controller?" "What assistance did you have once you had landed by parachute?" On and on they went until I could take no more. They released me and I collapsed onto the floor. A gruff command and the two guards who had brought me here took hold of me and half dragged, half carried me out of the room, back up the stairs and into my cell removing the hand and ankle cuffs before throwing me onto the floor. The cell door was slammed shut, and somehow I managed to get onto the bed where I passed out into a world of blackness.

I awoke to the sound of heavy footsteps marching along the corridor, becoming ever louder as they came nearer. How long had I been unconscious? Was it time for more torture and interrogation? I knew I couldn't take any more. The footsteps stopped directly outside my cell. The rattling and clinking of heavy keys being put into a lock, the lock being turned, and a heavy bolt being withdrawn, clanging as it was slid along the cell door, all meant to intimidate me no doubt. The door was opened just wide enough to allow the light from a small electric bulb to filter into the cell illuminating it from pitch-blackness. It must be nighttime then, but how long had it been since I was brought here? A day; a week? I had lost all track of time. My eyes were at first dazzled by this meagre light, but they gradually adjusted to it. The door was opened further and I could now make out the silhouettes of two black uniformed men standing menacingly in the doorway. As before each carried what appeared to be a truncheon in their hands, ready no doubt, to be used again at the slightest excuse.

One of them gruffly shouted to me, what he said I couldn't fully understand, it made no difference anyway. They strode over to me, the noise of the steel heels on their boots echoing off of the damp cold stone floor and around the walls of my tiny cell. Shouting at me again they roughly placed handcuffs and manacles on my hands and feet, cutting into my flesh as they did so, the blood warmly trickling over my limbs. They dragged me to my feet, whereupon I promptly collapsed onto the floor, my legs were so numb and weak from the beatings I had received that I had little feeling in them. Their hands roughly pulled me to my feet again and with a well-aimed truncheon blow to my head dragged me out of the cell and into the corridor, my bare feet scraping on the rough surface of the floor. More gruff commands which I didn't understand, and because I didn't immediately react to what they had shouted at me made them even more angry so they decided to roughen me up a bit more with a few well placed kicks from their highly polished Jack boots, laughing as they did so.

So it was to start all over again. Torture and questions until I told them what they wanted to hear. But then there was a sudden spark of an idea that entered my head. They believed me to be an agent of the SOE, very well then, why not tell them that I am. Why not? Could I convincingly lie to them and quickly make up a story that they would believe? We were getting nearer to the steps and the torture room, any moment now and I would be dragged down there to have more torture inflicted on me unless I could convince them that I was an SOE agent. We went on pass these steps, further down the corridor. What was happening now? What had they planned for me? Another method to extract information? As they dragged me along the dimly lit corridor I could hear the screams and cries for help from other unknown prisoners in the cells that I passed. I wondered if they too, were allied airmen that had been shot down and captured, and like me, brought here to be tortured and interrogated.

Stopping outside a room at the very end, one guard knocked sharply on its door. The door to this room appeared to be solid wood with several decorated wooden panels. Hearing no response from within he opened the door and pushed me through where upon I fell onto the floor. I raised myself up onto my elbows and was amazed to see that this room was very luxurious. It was well furnished with several leather chairs and a small, low table in the centre, with brightly coloured thick carpets and rugs on the floor. The walls were all panelled in a dark polished wood, at the far end a large stained glass window allowed sun light to penetrate, the colours of the glass lighting up the carpets into a more dazzling display of richness and opulence. Hanging from behind a richly carved desk was a large portrait of Adolf Hitler in his typical stern military pose. This I thought was very odd. I knew I must have killed Hitler, I saw his head disintegrate before my eyes and felt his hot blood on my face, so why display his portrait still?

The two guards picked me up and forced me to sit down in a chair facing the desk. With my hands again cuffed roughly behind my back I waited for my fate. Through bleary eyes I could see that a folder had been placed precisely in the centre of the desk. Was this yet another clever interrogation technique the Germans used? Torture first, and then kindness to obtain information? I was about to find out.

From a doorway to my right another German entered the room, he ordered the handcuffs to be removed before dismissing the guards with a contemptible wave of his hand. He was not in uniform, but wore a very smart pin striped double-breasted suit. In the jacket lapel was a single sprig of some kind of flower, pinned below he wore a small metal swastika badge. Slowly and purposely he walked across the room and over to the desk. Standing there for a second, he set his deep blue eyes firmly onto me. His short cropped blonde hair standing very erect on his head. So this was one of the master race! A blue eyed blonde, as Hitler and his henchmen of the Third Reich expected all pure Germans to be. Pulling the chair away from the desk he slowly sat down, his eyes still fixed upon me, observing me very closely for any response to show on my own bruised face. Opening a draw he pulled out a full packet of Players cigarettes and, opening the packet, leant across the desk, offering me one. Shaking my head I refused it. Taking a cigarette for himself, he placed it neatly into a cigarette holder he had produced from the same draw, and, almost as if it was part of a centuries old ritual, lit it with an ornamental gold cigarette lighter that was on the desk. Taking a deep inhale from the cigarette he slowly and deliberately blew the smoke up into the air above him and sat there watching it drift away until it disappeared towards the ceiling. All this was obviously done to intimidate me.

"Good afternoon 4264801 Flight Sergeant Andrew Harper. And how are you today? I trust you have been well looked after and your accommodation is satisfactory?"

Hearing him speak perfect English should have come as a surprise to me, but it didn't, after all, his sole purpose was to extract every detail of information from me; where I had found shelter; had I received help from any German citizen; but most importantly, how had I planned the assassination of Adolf Hitler. I must have surely have had assistance in accomplishing that, there was no way I could have been successful without some sort of help. In his mind he couldn't possibly accept that I was acting alone and that circumstances were such that I was in the right place and at the right time. Did I say anything to the other interrogators in my confusion that they now felt that another approach was needed or had they indeed finished with me and at long last I was to be sent to a prisoner of war camp?

Looking down at the desk he slowly opened up the document folder in front of him as if to make it perfectly clear to me that he was in total control and time was on his side. Taking out several sheets of paper he read them slowly one by one, picking each one up by the corner, carefully turning the page over while inhaling on his Players cigarette, blowing the smoke up into the air. Satisfying him self with whatever the papers contained he carefully closed the folder. What was to happen to me now? I had no illusions that my life was in his well-manicured hands.

" Let's see now. Ah, yes. We know all about you 4264801 Flight Sergeant Harper, Lancaster bomber pilot. Shot down by our glorious Luftwaffe on the night of 4th November, but unfortunately you were the only survivor from your aircraft. The rest of your crew sadly perished, but you must already know that. You are quite obviously a very brave young man, but we believe that all is not as it seems. You see we believe that you are not whom you claim to be, you are not a flier, you are in fact an agent of the English terrorist organisation the SOE. Your false identity is nothing more than a very clever cover story conceived by your masters in England for just such a mission as this. You were meant to be parachuted into Germany from a Lancaster bomber during one of your nightly terror attacks. This of course gave, you hoped, some credence to your cover story of being shot down. Unfortunately for you, our glorious Luftwaffe shot your bomber down in flames." He couldn't possibly believe that I was an SOE agent, parachuted into the heart of Germany for the sole purpose of assassinating Hitler.

Sitting back into his chair, he looked straight across at me, his eyes focused on mine. "You are not a flyer in the English Bomber Command, but an agent sent on a mission to kill the Fuhrer. There is no point in continuing with your ridiculous story, it will achieve nothing, better to admit to your crime and confess now."

His words jolted me to my very core. This was absolute rubbish. They must be aware that I am in the Royal Air Force. My uniform and identity tag proves that. If I am to be treated as an enemy agent then my situation is untenable. There would be no protection for me under the Geneva Convention. As far as the Germans are concerned I am an enemy agent dressed in the uniform of a senior NCO in the RAF and therefore will be treated as such, a spy and an assassin.

"You see Flight Sergeant Harper, you have made things very difficult for us! Do we acknowledge that you are indeed who you claim to be and accord you protection as a prisoner of war under the Geneva Convention, or do we say that you are a professional assassin in the employment of the SOE and have you shot as such accordingly? If I decide that you are in fact to be treated as a prisoner of war I cannot possibly send you to one of our prisoner of war Stalags, as a 'normal' prisoner of war can I now? After all, you have succeeded where many others have failed. Yes, Flight Sergeant Harper, you assassinated our beloved Fuhrer. So what am I to do with you then? You do understand the problem that I have? But you see your assassination has been quite pointless. Steps are already in place to keep this tragedy from the German people, and the Fuhrer, as far as they are concerned, is alive and very well!

"We Germans are a clever race Flight Sergeant, but you will never be in a position to find out how we have achieved this. Heinrich Himmler has taken a very special interest in your capture. He and his SS have now taken full control of the Third Reich. And as for you, you are no longer of any interest to us. You are to be sent to a special camp where you will be kept until Germany is victorious, as we surely will be. We have already informed the Red Cross of your tragic death along with the rest of your gallant but foolish crew. You are going to one of our 'special' camps, Dachau Concentration Camp in fact, where you will 'disappear' forever! Nobody will know who you are or what you have done. You will be segregated from our other 'guests' at the camp and you will be have a special code against you name - NN - or 'Nacht und Nebel', which means in English 'Night and Fog'. Simply put, you will disappear forever into the night and the fog of the glorious Third Reich. You will never be heard of again, disappearing into the darkness for all time. So, goodbye, Flight Sergeant Harper. For you, the war really is truly over."

The door behind me opened. Looking up from his desk he looked surprised to see who had just entered the room. He immediately rose up from his desk and stood briskly to attention giving the Nazi salute.

"Reich Fuhrer Himmler. I am very privileged and honoured to meet you," he said in a nervous yet admiring voice.

Himmler? The head of the SS - here? From a corner of my eye the figure of a man came steadily into view. Moving past me he stood in front of the desk, his hands clasped in front of him, looking down at me from behind his thick-rimmed glasses. "I have come to see for myself the Royal Air Force terror flyer who murdered our beloved Fuhrer. I take it that you have now finished your questioning?"

"Yes Reich Fuhrer. And I have, as you have ordered, informed him as to his fate. Everything is in place for his immediate transfer to Dachau."

"Excellent. You have done very well. You're service to the new German leadership will not go un-noticed. Stand up man!" He was addressing me now. I stood up, standing face to face with the man who controlled not only the SS but the Gestapo as well. So this man had decided my fate. Immaculately dressed in his black SS uniform, his eyes piercing at me through his glasses. I looked back at him, my eyes directly looking into his eyes, my last act of defiance to him and the Third Reich. His eyes turned away, looking instead towards the man at the desk, turning his back on me.

"So this is an English terror bomber. I was expecting much more." His voice now changed, sounding much more threatening. "You will now forget everything that you know. No details of this case must ever be heard outside of these walls. All records are to be securely sealed and stored in this building, clearly marked for my personal attention only. I will hold you personally responsible for seeing to it. If you or any of your staff should ever mention this man's name or tell of his fate, then you and your family, and their families, will be eliminated, and I will personally see to that! Is that clearly understood?"

Looking over to my interrogator I could see that he was visibly shaking, small beads of sweat were trickling down the side of his now very white face. Now he was in fear of his own life, poetic justice. "I fully under Herr Reich Fuhrer."

"Very well then. I now order that this man vanishes forever. If I ever hear of him again or hear his name mentioned by anyone then the punishment will be carried out immediately, that I promise. He must vanish now from the world and be lost for ever within the Third Reich."

The other man nodded, stood to attention, clicking his heels as he did so and smartly gave the Nazi salute. Himmler responded and, turning on the heels of his highly polished boots was gone from the room as quickly as he had appeared.

Having composed himself he sat down behind the desk and he spoke his final words to me. "Flight Sergeant Harper. You have heard the Reich Fuhrer. You will now be transported to Dachau Concentration Camp. You have ceased to exist from this moment on. Nobody will ever speak to you again under pain of death, if you attempt to communicate by any method you will be shot. Death would be an easy way out for you; you will suffer your fate for the rest of your life. Nobody will ever know who you are and why you are classed as 'Nacht und Nebel'. Your files, here in front of me, will be stored away into the very depths of Gestapo Headquarters here in Berlin to be forgotten about and only fit for gathering dust."

With these last words he rose from the desk, smiling at me with an evil grin that displayed his gold teeth. Pressing a buzzer on the desktop the two guards entered the room and strode over to me where they roughly bundled me out of the room, laughing grotesquely as they did so. I was manhandled into another room. More gruff commands. They were pointing to a set of very old and soiled looking clothes and then back to my now tattered RAF uniform. Looking at these 'new' clothes they reminded me of the striped pyjamas I used to wear as a child. But I knew that these were anything but as innocent. So I was to change into these, and by wearing them my identity as 4264801 Flight Sergeant Harper, Royal Air Force, was being eradicated in the process. I noticed the initials 'NN' clearly marked in bold red letters on the jacket and trousers. There was also a pair of old wooden clogs that I had to wear.

Once I had changed into these foul smelling clothes the guards manacled my hands behind my back, and just to make sure that I would not make a last dash for freedom they manacled my ankles. These had heavy chains attached to them that were then fitted securely to the handcuffs, making it impossible for me to take but the shortest of steps.

I was frogged marched along the corridor and up several flights of cold stone steps, leaving behind me the screams of other prisoners. This time I was taken out through the rear exit of the building and pushed towards a German Army truck parked just outside of the door. Somehow, I'm not sure how, I managed to climb up the tailgate to collapse in a heap onto the floor. Inside through the dim light I could see two SS guards waiting there for me. Grabbing my arms they threw me into one corner, the tailgate was slammed shut, the sound of the lorry's engine came to life and we were moving. My next stop would be Dachau Concentration Camp, where, no doubt, at some time I would die.

As far as the Third Reich was concerned, I had just ceased to exist. Himmler, the SS and the Gestapo had seen to that.

Chapter 5

Forty years on

The letter arrived in the early morning post. Picking it up from the hall carpet I noticed that it had a German postmark and was addressed to my mother. I placed it on a breakfast tray and took it through to the garden of her cottage in Wickenby, Lincolnshire, with her breakfast of toast and marmalade and a pot of tea where she was enjoying the warmth of the summer's early morning sun. After the war had ended she decided to remain in the same cottage she had briefly shared with her husband – my father - before he went off on his last operation that fateful night in 1941. This is where she could cast her mind back and remember those happy days when they were both together. She felt close to him here in these familiar surroundings.

She had been unwell lately. "Just old age" the doctor had said. Although in her 70th year she still had the youthful looks of a much younger woman. But we both knew that her life was rapidly drawing to an end. Our family doctor had done all that was possible to ease her pain from the cancer that had spread through her now frail body. But there was one pain that no medicine could ever stop, that was the emotional pain of loosing he beloved husband at such a young age. It had been some 40 odd years since she received the news from the Air Ministry via the Red Cross that her husband had been killed in action flying over Germany along with all of his crew in the Lancaster bomber he was piloting during the Second World War.

She had watched his aircraft take off in the darkening sky from his base in Wickenby unaware that that would be the last time she would ever see him. In the Station Operations Room each Lancaster was recorded on a status board as to its time of departure and time of landing. Against 'G' George, written in white chalk, were the words 'Overdue.' As the hours passed away and no reports came in of an 'away landing' at another airfield 'G' George's name was wiped from the board. Being so long overdue it was now assumed that the aircraft had 'been lost', probably shot down, and had crashed over enemy occupied Europe, where there might be some hope of the crew surviving, or of coming down in the dark, cold water of the North Sea where survival was less likely.

He and his crew were first listed as 'missing in action' as all missing airmen are until the facts could be proved otherwise. Then that final telegram or letter of condolence and sympathy stating that the Air Ministry had finally had confirmation from the International Red Cross via the German authorities that her husband was in fact dead. Killed alongside his crew when their Lancaster crashed into a pine forest returning from the target that night. Only her husband's body was missing and had not been recovered for burial by the Germans, the remains of the rest of the crew were buried together in a nearby churchyard.

She looked up from her chair as I handed her the letter, raising her hands to shade her eyes from the bright morning sun. Taking it in her frail hand, she placed it first on her lap and then onto the tabletop to open later not really showing any great interest in it. I poured out her tea and sitting down beside her I mentioned the post-mark to her, asking if she knew anybody in Germany who might want to write to her. Looking puzzled she picked it up and carefully slit the envelope open removing the letter, unfolding it.

Holding it in her hands I could see that it was written in a very clear, if shaking hand, and in very good English. Reading from it aloud to me her voice became quite shaky as she read it, her hands were now trembling. I took it from her and began to read it aloud to her.

My dear Mrs. Harper,

Forgive me for taking so many years to write to you, but with the passage of time I found it more and more difficult to do so, but at long last I have found the courage to put pen to paper. I hope this letter reaches you, not being really sure if I have your correct address, which I obtained with the very kind help of the International Red Cross.

After much soul searching I have decided that now was the time to pass on to you certain information as to the true circumstances of your husband, Flight Sergeant Andrew Harper's, last days in captivity during the Second World War in Germany.

My mother's hand started to shake uncontrollably upon hearing this. She looked at me with a look of total disbelief in her eyes. Like my mother, I couldn't really comprehend on what the content of this letter was saying. I read on, reading the letter more slowly now, speaking as if in some strange dream, not really believing exactly what was written on every page. Last days in captivity? Did the letter writer have the correct airman here? My father was killed in action; he couldn't possibly have been a prisoner of war. That couldn't possibly be true.

> *Please prepare yourself for what I know will be a great shock to you. Your husband was not killed when his bomber was shot down over Germany. He was actually captured and imprisoned in Dachau Concentration Camp by the SS. He spent the last years of the war there following his interrogation at Gestapo Headquarters in Berlin in 1941. I am so very sorry to have to tell you that the SS executed him at Dachau in the very last days of the war. I know this as a fact, you see, I was possibly the last person to see him alive.*

Executed? But that must be wrong. The International Red Cross had officially informed my mother that he was killed when his Lancaster had crashed after being shot down. His body was never found, but there can be no doubt about his fate. The letter went on….

> *I know this to be true. You see, I too was imprisoned in Dachau and came to know your husband, if only for a few short days, while I was imprisoned there. There were many stories and rumours within the camp as to who he was and why he was sent there and not, as he should have been, to a prisoner of war camp. You see, it was strictly forbidden to have any contact with him as he was declared as being 'NN' or 'Nacht und*

Nebel' which in English translates as 'Night and Fog', a prisoner, lost within the Third Reich forever more. But there are ways and means if you are brave enough of talking to such prisoners. One or two prisoners, myself amongst them, discovered by befriending him without the German guards finding out, that he was in fact the pilot of a Lancaster bomber, but had been declared 'Nacht und Nebel' for some crime he had committed against the Third Reich.Buried deep within the archives at the museum at Dachau are documents that revealed what really happened to your husband and why he was there. I made it my quest after the war had ended, to prove that all of what your husband had told me in those last few days of his life could be proved.

I'm afraid that I am too old to travel to England, but your husband talked to me of his son. Please, I beg of you. If your son can come to Germany I will disclose the whole story to him. Your husband, your son's father, was a truly very brave man. What he did should be told to the entire world. The proof is here, and I have it. I do not want to disclose too much at this stage for fear that you will consider me to be 'a crank', but I can assure you that I am not. All I seek is that you and your son should be made aware of the truth surrounding your husband's last days and the circumstances surrounding his death.

Apart from a few very close friends who have helped me to investigate I have told no one else about your husband. You should be the first to know. I can be contacted at the address on this letter. Please contact me as soon as you can. I ask for no payment or reward of any kind. I gave a solemn oath to your husband in Dachau that I would do all in my power to ensure that his story will be made known to you and, if you should wish, the whole world.

His story is far bigger and important than you can ever imagine. It must be told to 'put history' right.

Yours with the greatest respect,

Gert Winkler.

Could all of this be really true? My father, executed in a Nazi concentration camp, and not killed when his Lancaster was shot down that fateful night over Germany. Had the entire last 40 years been a lie?

Looking at me with puzzled eyes I passed the letter back to my mother. She carefully placed it back into the envelope and turned to me, tears welling up in her eyes. She was visibly shaken by what the letter contained. Taking her hand in mine I consoled her as best I could. The contents of the letter and what this man claimed were a shock to me, so how must she be feeling? A look of utter confusion appeared on her face as she looked to me for some kind of re-assurance. I spoke to her gently, trying to calm her and put her at ease. Slowly she regained her dignity as the contents of the letter began to sink into her mind. But what to do now? We needed time to consider this letter and its implications. I picked it up with the envelope and read it over again for myself. It was a fantastic claim to make. But just who was this mysterious Herr Winkler?

My mother asked to be taken indoors where she could sit in her favourite easy chair in the front room. Helping her carefully to her feet, I supported her while she made her faltering and unsteady way back into the house seeking the comfort of her old chair. She sat there for a while saying nothing, but just looking at the photographs of my father which adorned the sideboard next to her chair, tears in her old eyes rolling steadily down her wrinkled cheeks.

The old black and white photographs were quite faded by now. Taken during wartime Britain, they were not of a good quality, but I could still clearly see almost all of the features on my father's face. There was several of him in his best blue uniform that proudly displayed the pilot wings on his jacket. Some included his crew photographed in the local Inn next to the airfield where he was stationed. The most important of all though was the wedding photograph taken outside of the church. This is the one that my mother cherished most.

I didn't know what else I could say to her just now, so I went into the kitchen and switched the kettle on. What is it that we British do in such circumstances - make a cup of tea and take the time to think about the situation? I put a fresh cup of strong, sweet tea onto the coffee table just in front of her where she could easily reach it, although I was sure that she really wasn't aware of me placing it there. She was really deep in thought over the contents of this letter.

At last she spoke to me. "Andrew," for I was named after my father, "you must go and meet this man and find out from him what he knows. There is no reason why he should write to us after all these years if he didn't know the truth surrounding your father's death. You must go and find out." I looked at her with some surprise. Her voice was very strong and determined. I hadn't heard her speak like this for many a year, such was the effect the letter had upon her. "You're right mother of course. I must contact him from the details he gave of himself."

His letter gave not only an address but also a phone number, so without any further thought I went into the hall, picked up the telephone and rang his number not really knowing if he would be at the other end of the line, or what exactly I would say to him. After what seemed an age somebody picked up the receiver at the other end and spoke in German. For a few seconds I remained speechless not knowing what to say, recovering I said in English, that I wished to speak with Herr Winkler, hoping that they would understand what I was saying - my German being non-existent! The voice then spoke in near perfect English saying that I was talking to Herr Winkler and how could he be of help. I think I was functioning on nerves and the surreal atmosphere that I found myself in. I quickly introduced myself and briefly went over the contents of his letter.

I noticed a distinct wavering in his voice, almost as if he was gently crying. Without further ado he suggested that I should fly to Germany, meet with him, and then he would show me the evidence of his claim and tell me the real truth of my father's last days on earth. Asking him for more details he gave his apologies saying that it was far too complex to give answers over a phone line. So it was agreed there and then. I would fly to Germany the very next day to meet him.

I went back to my mother who was sipping from the cup of tea, her hands still trembling. There were tears in her eyes, and when she looked up at me I didn't have to speak a word. She could tell by some sort of mother's instinct that I would be going to Germany, all I had to say was that it would be the next day. A slight nod of her head signified her understanding and agreement. She took my hand and gave it the gentlest of squeezes.

Now I had to make sure my mother would be looked after while I was away. I went back to the hall and phoned a very good friend of ours who lived just a few doors away and briefly explained to her about the letter and its contents, asking if she could look after my mother while I was away in Germany which she gladly agreed to do. My mother had met her at our local branch of the Royal British Legion and had been very good friends with her for many years. Her father had also served in the Royal Air Force during the Second World War and had recently died, so they both had a common interest.

So, with the arrangements for my mother finalised I booked a flight to Munich for the following morning, where the mysterious Herr Winkler would meet me. Tomorrow I would know more, and then perhaps some sense could be made of the whole affair. I promised my mother that I would discover the truth and that I would meet this man, to listen to what he had to say, and examine the evidence he had claimed to have discovered. His letter said was that my father wasn't killed in action but was executed in a concentration camp. He gave no hint as to the circumstances either in his letter or during my phone call to him.

Our neighbour arrived a few hours later to stay for a few days after explaining all that she knew to her husband who was only to happy for his wife to help out, after all they were only a few doors away from each other so he would be close at hand if need be. We really were lucky to have such good neighbours as this. Knowing that my mother would now be in very good hands I arranged for a taxi to take me to the main line train station so that I could travel down to London for an overnight stay, and then in the morning travelling on to Heathrow to catch my flight to Munich. I quickly packed an overnight bag and I was ready to go.

Chapter 6

Munich & Dachau Concentration Camp

I arrived in plenty of time at Heathrow. I didn't sleep very well during the night, there were too many wild thoughts running riot in my head. Herr Winkler claimed that he was after no reward of any kind. What had my father supposed to have done that this man had taken years of his life to investigate and provide the evidence for? Today I hoped I would have the answers to these questions and many more.

The airport tannoy system sprang into life announcing that all passengers for my flight should make their way to passport control and check in prior to boarding the aircraft. Entering the aircraft cabin I wondered how my father and his crew felt each time they climbed aboard their Lancaster bomber to attack Germany. Would they return safely from this mission to have to go through it all again the following night, or would they be shot down as so many Bomber Command crews were? Life expectancy for aircrew was very short; most were lost on their first 'trip' while others - the few - completed two tours, a tour being thirty operational missions.

Settling down for the short flight in a comfortable seat, the stewardess offered refreshments for the flight, a lot different from my father's experience flying heavy four engine bombers. The best those crews could expect was a flask of coffee or soup and a sandwich or two. No comfortable seats for them either, sitting for hours on end in the confines of the various crew positions. I tried to put these thoughts out of my head, but I thought it strange that for some years now I had never ever really considered what these brave young men endured so that we today, could enjoy our freedom, that they had given their lives for; a very sobering thought. It was a quick uneventful flight from London Heathrow Airport and I arrived at Munich International Airport on a bright summer's morning where I was to be met by the mysterious Herr Winkler.

I made way with other passengers through the 'Arrivals' gate into the vast hall beyond, there I anxiously scanned the faces of the crowd gathered who were waiting for friends, husbands, or wives to appear from the doorway. From the edge of this crowd of people I noticed my name scrawled in heavy black capital letters onto a piece of cardboard. This must surely be Herr Winkler. I waved to him indicating that I had seen him and walked over to greet him.

He looked a lot older than I had imagined him to be, his face was very drawn and deeply wrinkled giving the impression of a much older man, his eyes were bright but sunken deeply into their sockets. I recalled in his letter that he was imprisoned in Dachau so his appearance was possibly due to his incarceration there during the war. Standing at about five feet two inches tall, he was small in stature although he stood very erect and stiff backed. He was dressed in a cheap looking, but smart dark grey suit and wore a slightly battered old trilby hat, tilting to one side on his head. I introduced myself to him and he greeted me warmly with a firm handshake and spoke to me in near perfect English.

"Herr Harper. I am so glad that you decided to come and I'm so very happy to meet you at long last after all of these years. Did you have a pleasant flight?"

Not waiting for an answer he carried on talking, at the same time offering to take my small piece of hand luggage from me, which I politely declined. For such an old gentleman he certainly had bags of energy and zest, which proves the point about pre-judging people from the initial contact.

"I have a good friend of mine waiting outside to take us to our hotel on the outskirts of Munich. We can talk on the way and I can properly introduce myself to you." Without further ado he turned around and hurriedly walked off towards the airport exit taking hold of my elbow and ushering me quickly along. Herr Winkler certainly appeared not to be a man of few words. I just hoped that he would be as talkative when we could finally sit down properly and discuss the full story of what he had discovered about my father's death.

"Herr Harper, this is my friend Ernst who has very kindly offered to be our driver while you are staying here in Germany."

"Gudentag Herr Harper." Ernst greeted me with a warm handshake opening the car door for me. He was a much younger man than the mysterious Herr Winkler, perhaps no older than 40. Ernst then took my hand luggage and placed it in the boot of the car, Herr Winkler motioned me into the rear seat while he sat in the front passenger seat alongside Ernst.

Ernst's car was a black Volkswagen Golf. I thought it strange, that, looking at it, this was probably the only good thing that had survived from the Third Reich and Nazi regime - the illustrious Volkswagen - or 'the peoples car'. This was the car that Adolf Hitler had wanted every German family to own, to use on the new autobahn system that the Third Reich had constructed for its people, using the conscripted labour of the many thousands of un-employed Germans to achieve a superb network of roads, which would be used to transport troops and tank transporters at the time of Germany's intention to 'free' the Austrian people and invade Poland which would start the Second World War when England and France declared war on Germany two days after the German invasion of Poland on September 1 1939.

The drive to the hotel was short and uneventful, the traffic in Munich being as congested as London, but it did flow very freely without too many frustrating hold ups. Ernst pulled off of the main road and onto the hotel forecourt, stopping outside the entrance, smartly moving to the rear of his car, he opened the boot and handed me my overnight bag. With a firm handshake he spoke to Herr Winkler before getting back into the car and driving off.

From the outside the hotel had the appearance of being pre-war, timber beamed frontage with white brickwork. From the guttering above were several ancient carved wooden figures lending a gothic feeling to the hotel's surrounds. The roof was constructed of thick wooden tiles, again, obviously dating back a number of years. This must have been one of the few buildings that survived the bombing of Munich relatively unscathed. We entered through two panelled wooden doors that were already open and then through a double plate glass door into the air-conditioned reception area. At the reception desk a very pretty young girl booked us both in and handed us our room keys, I noticed that she was dressed in a typical Bavarian dress and blouse which suited the hotel, anything more modern would have been badly out of place and not in keeping with the décor or atmosphere inside.

Herr Winkler now suggested that we meet in the bar after settling ourselves into our respective rooms. We made our way towards a narrow flight of stairs; being quite a small hotel, we didn't have the luxury of an elevator, and there were only two floors to contend with anyway. Finding my room I quickly unpacked the few clothes I had brought for my short stay in Munich. Before I went down to the bar I read his letter once more, still finding it difficult to comprehend its full meaning and implications. The only way to find out was to hear what Herr Winkler had to say. Folding his letter up I replaced it in the envelope, placing it in my jacket pocket and locking the door to my room, made my way back to the lobby and bar. I was anxious to question him to discover what he knew and how he had obtained whatever information he had.

At the bar I ordered, in my best schoolboy German, a good German beer, the first I had ever tasted. Fortunately for me and my extremely poor German the barman spoke almost perfect English which put my attempt at speaking in his native tongue to shame. He carefully poured the beer into a tall glass, placed it onto a tray and led me to a table away from the bar. Herr Winkler had not yet arrived so I sat down in a very comfortable leather chair, the barman placed the glass on the table and asking if there was anything else that I required, turned and walked away. Looking at the glass I could see droplets of water running slowly down its side, joining up with others and producing a larger rivulet until it reached the tabletop. Lifting it up I took my first cautious sip of genuine German beer. Savouring it slowly in my mouth I found much to my surprise to be a much stronger but smoother taste than those German beer imports back in England, slowly swallowing it to enjoy its strong but very pleasant taste. I placed the now half full glass onto the table, feeling just a bit more at ease.

Looking about me the hotel looked as if it had definitely been built in the early 1900's as I thought. It still retained that 'picture postcard' look, with low wooden ceiling beams and several arches that separated smaller drinking areas in the lounge. These arches were highly decorated with carved wooden gothic like figures and different kinds of intricately carved wild flowers and leaves. There was a mixture of plastered and granite stone walls, and highly polished well-worn stone slabs on the floor. The walls that were plastered were decorated with painted groups of grape vines and also young boys and girls dressed in traditional Bavarian clothes of the pre-war era.

There were a few other people, tourists I assumed, in the bar sitting at other tables, either talking or pouring over various tourist leaflets planning their days out in Bavaria. What a difference it must have been during the 1930's. I could easily imagine this room being filled with young fanatical Germans' celebrating and drinking to the health of Adolf Hitler before and during the Second World War, and on reflection, to the Kaiser and the Imperial Germany of the Great War of 1914 to 1918. I found it difficult to understand how an entire nation could have been so entranced and mesmerised by such a ruthless man. Recalling my history lessons from my school days we were told that at the end of the First World War the German Nation never considered that it had in fact, been defeated by the Allies. The German Army was never finally defeated in battle, but marched back to Germany still intact as a fighting force with its arms and equipment after the Armistice of November 11th 1918. This propaganda was taught to the youth of Germany and that, together with the financial retributions placed on Germany by the Allies, high unemployment and daily food riots on the streets, became the foundation stones for the forming of the Nazi Party and the rise to power of Adolf Hitler. Two World Wars, and for what? Will the human race never learn! If only I could turn the clock back and correct all of those early mistakes, what would the world be like now I wondered?

I was rapidly brought back to the present when I recognised the voice of Herr Winkler ordering a drink from the bar. Looking towards him he acknowledged my presence and with drink in hand, walked over sitting down in the chair opposite mine.

"Herr Harper. I hope you have settled in and find your room comfortable. The staff here are extremely helpful so please feel free to use the services as you wish." As if to give himself a short pause and time to think he took a long drink from his glass, slowly placing it onto the table. Looking at me squarely in the face he spoke. "Can I say that what I am about to tell you is an incredible story about your very courageous father. There will be moments when you will find it hard to believe what I will tell you. You will think that I am some kind of a crank who has, for some obscure reason, made this story up to gain something from you. But I can assure you that what you are about to hear is perfectly true. I will start from the very beginning and tell you exactly what your father did and how he died."

So this was to be the time when at long last I would discover the real truth behind my father's death. I slowly raised my glass to my lips taking a long drink from it. Emptying the glass I placed it on the table in front of me, and attracting the attention of a young waitress I ordered two more glasses for us.

"First, let me start by telling you how I met your father. I was sent to Dachau Concentration Camp in April of 1945, just 6 days before the American Army liberated it. I firmly believe that the only reason I survived when many tens of thousands, including your father, died, was because time was on my side and the Germans knew that all was lost, their mighty Third Reich was rapidly collapsing around their feet. The Germans knew the camp would be liberated soon and were busy destroying documents to prevent them from falling into Allied hands where they would be used to punish members of the camp administrators, doctors, and guards, both male and female, all of whom were extremely brutal and fanatical Nazis, dedicated to Adolf Hitler, the Nazi Party and the Third Reich.

"These Germans were fanatical about keeping accurate records and it was these very same records that were used against them as evidence at the War Crimes trials at Nuremberg. Fortunately not all of these records were destroyed in time, there were just too many of them. Many survived the efforts to burn them and after an initial investigation by the Allied powers, were deposited in a place of safety where they were filed and stored for future reference. Many of the camp guards had already deserted, throwing away their uniforms and changing into civilian clothes in an effort to evade being caught by the advancing American army and being brought to justice for the atrocities they had committed over the long years. Those that had not escaped in time discarded their uniforms and wore the clothing taken from the dead prisoners in the vain hope that they would be mistaken as survivors. Thankfully however, this did not work. They were too well fed to pass off as inmates. Many were later identified by survivors who recognised them and pointed them out from special parades. Some of the guards that decided to stay opted for another ploy, suddenly 'switching sides' and began to treat us much better - no more beatings and even giving us food - in a last ditch effort to gain favour with the Americans and hope to trick them into believing that they were in fact 'decent' SS guards, forced to carry out their orders, but the Americans were not fooled, we, the inmates, soon pointed these monsters out and told them the undeniable truth.

"But how did I end up in Dachau? I was sent there because I had dared to openly criticise the Fuhrer and had been overheard by a member of the Hitler Youth, you know, those brain washed children who believed that Adolf Hitler was a God and chosen to lead the German people to world domination. Yes, even in 1945 when the war had long ago been lost there were still those die-hard Nazis who believed that Germany could win the war using Hitler's much vaunted 'super weapons'. There were many such people in Germany who held the same views as I did, even from before the war started in 1939, that Hitler and the Nazi Party would only bring more trouble and greater problems for the German people.

"As a student I joined the 'White Rose' student organisation to oppose the regime. Many of my student friends were also members, distributing anti Nazi leaflets in public places that we printed in great secrecy. The Gestapo caught many and these were sent to concentration camps or executed after so called trials, some of my friends among them. One of them I will never ever forget, a young student - Sophie Scholl. We were both students at the same university and I was madly in love with her, she didn't know that of course, she already had a long-standing boy friend. Sophie and her brother Hans, along with five other White Rose members were found guilty of distributing anti Nazi leaflets on the 22nd of February 1943, and were condemned to death by the so called People's Court.

"The Reich Minister of Justice could have pardoned her for this very petty so-called crime, but did not intervene. A little after five o'clock on the same afternoon that sentence was passed, Sophie was taken away and beheaded along with her brother and five others. Twelve others were given long prison terms. One White Rose member, Helmth von Moltke escaped and made his way to England via Scandinavia, where news of these atrocities were publicised.

"In the middle of 1943 millions of leaflets were dropped over Germany by the Royal Air Force, they were titled 'A German Tract; Munich Students' Manifesto'. Yes Herr Harper, many, many young Germans were strongly opposed to Nazi Germany, and paid with their own lives. It is no coincidence that I asked you to fly to Munich, for in this very hotel during the war, is where Sophie, her brother and I would meet with other like-minded students". At this point he paused for a while, allowing me to take in what he had just told me.

I sat there dumbfounded, what could I say to Herr Winkler after this disclosure. Here, sitting before me, was a member of a wartime anti Nazi movement, the White Rose. Any doubts I had about his sincerity were now well and truly dispelled. He continued.

"Germany was a nation where neighbours didn't trust each other. If you spoke up against Hitler, who could you trust - nobody. Many that did speak against Hitler and the Nazi party were denounced, as I was, and were, how shall I put it, eliminated. Arrested during the night never to be heard of again.

"I considered myself much more fortunate than many of my fellow students. The Gestapo had no evidence that I ever belonged to the 'White Rose' movement and so I was only charged as being 'a threat to the German Nation.' After my arrest I was put on trial by the very same 'People's Court' that had condemned Sophie to death two years earlier. I was sentenced to 15 years hard labour in Dachau. Along with many others I was then transported to the camp by train, not in passenger carriages but in overcrowded and filthy cattle trucks, where many of my companions did not survive the journey.

"We were so crowded in that there was no room for any of us to sit down; we had to stand shoulder to shoulder for many, many hours without a break of any kind. We were not given any food or water during the long train journey. Can you begin to imagine the state of the wagon and us by the time we arrived? The dead and dying crammed in so tight that they could not fall to the floor. The smell of excrement on each and every one of us spread all over the carriage, on the walls and floor. A cattle truck designed to hold eight cows now holding 50, 60 and even 70 human beings.

"This is how the Nazis treated its own people who had 'stepped out of line'. When we eventually arrived, I, with hundreds of others that had survived the journey were force marched the short distance from the railway trucks, through the camp gates, past the guardroom and into the camp. The dead and dying were left behind in the wagons to be removed by other inmates from the camp where they were piled onto handcarts to be burnt in the ovens. I will always remember the words 'Arbiet Macht Frei' which were set above the iron gates as a 'greeting' to us all - 'Work sets you Free'. Once inside it was plainly obvious to see there was total chaos all around. Prisoners were wandering aimlessly about, not taking any notice of us new arrivals, after all, why should they? Thousands had arrived in the same way now for many years.

"I could see in front of me two rows of about forty single storey wooden barracks which were crammed to overflowing with thousands of starving prisoners, dressed in what I can only describe as rags, many were obviously near to death. Their starved bodies were just skeletons, covered in skin and very little flesh. Some were dead, lying alongside the barrack walls or in the gutters and pathways, totally ignored by other prisoners

"There seemed to be little if any discipline by the sadistic guards who took great pleasure in pushing and herding us in the direction of the barracks. Many of us were beaten with clubs for the slightest reason. A few more died in just this short walk, falling to the side of the road and left where they lay.

"We were driven along like cattle down the 'Lagerstrasse' - the main camp road dividing the two rows of barracks - this was lined with poplar trees, planted by the first 'political' prisoners when the camp was built in the early 1930's. I decided that if I was to survive I must quickly get away from this crowd and try to mix in with the other 'older' prisoners. Seizing the moment when the guards were distracted, I quickly slipped away from the column, and moving with some difficulty, managed to force my way amongst the other inmates, creeping through one of the filthy over crowded barracks.

"Fortunately none of the guards had spotted me make my break. I made my way past the other prisoners, a few of them reaching out with their skeletal arms begging me for food and help as I brushed past their pathetic bodies. Finally reaching a far corner of the squalid room I came across a solitary figure whose appearance and dress was different to the other prisoners. He was wearing the same ragged and dirty striped clothing but with the addition of a bright red circle and the letters 'NN' sewn boldly onto the coat and trousers. I wondered why the others were keeping away from him; there was little enough space to spare, so why was this prisoner being treated like a leper?

"He looked up at me as I came nearer to him. From his appearance he must have been here for many years, but he still had that look of absolute defiance and hatred for these sadistic Germans in his gaunt and black-rimmed eyes that were sunken into their sockets. I sat down beside him which must have been totally unexpected by him as he shuffled further away along the rough wooden bench. I tried to show him that I meant no harm to him and very gradually he began to trust me, although any quick movement on my part would immediately make him cringe away, not because he feared me I felt, but he seemed to genuinely fear for my own safety for being with him and attempting to talk to him. Looking back towards the others in the hut for their reactions to my act of what I considered to be kindness I was surprised to discover that they were totally ignoring us and keeping their distance, clearly not wanting to be involved with what I was doing.

"Ignoring any thoughts for myself I spoke to him slowly and he quietly acknowledged me. Seeing me wearing normal clothing as opposed to his own filthy uniform must obviously have made him very distrustful of me. After all I had suddenly appeared as if by magic. Perhaps he thought it was a trick of some kind. It was very obvious that he was in fear of his life. He had shackles on his wrists and ankles that had caused terrible cuts and sores to his limbs. The Germans were certainly making sure that there would be no escaping for him from this terrible place, but even if he could get rid of the shackles it was plainly obvious that he was far too weak to walk any distance. I slowly started a conversation with him, but his German was not at all very good. I was shocked when he spoke in English, which was plainly his first language. As my English was so much better than his German we spoke in his native tongue.

"In a weak and trembling voice he went on to tell me of a fantastic, if not unbelievable story of who he was and why the Gestapo, and Heinrich Himmler, leader the SS, had taken so much trouble to ensure his captivity. This man, your father, was claiming to have assassinated Adolf Hitler in 1941! I believe now, that he knew he would not survive the war and had to tell somebody what he had done before it was too late. It was, in many ways, a miracle that I had been sent here. Divine intervention by God? Who can tell? We spoke together in hushed voices for hours. He would stop every now and again as if he was finding it very difficult to recall all of the events that had led to him being imprisoned here."

I couldn't believe what Herr Winkler had just said. My father was claiming to have killed Adolf Hitler! No, there must be some mistake. Had this man, if indeed, he was my father, become insane? The whole world knew that Hitler had committed suicide deep within his bunker in Berlin just before the Soviet army captured the city in 1945, his body and that of Eve Braun had been discovered by Russian troops in the Reich Chancellery garden outside of the bunker.

"Like you must be now, I at first was very, very, sceptical about this man's claim. But he went on and told me of bailing out of his crippled Lancaster bomber, his good friends in his crew, their very names even. Then of his escape, hiding and sheltering in the deep pine forests and literally stumbling upon Hitler's retreat at Berchtesgaden. He described in great detail what he had seen there and how he had shot the Fuhrer with a pistol he had taken from one of the guards he had killed. He also spoke of his wife and new born son in England, - you - and made me vow that if I survived the war that I would contact them with the truth."

Imprisoned in Dachau was this man, undoubtedly English, who not only claimed to have assassinated Hitler, but who was also claiming to be my father! I looked at my empty glass on the table. I needed another drink. Attracting the attention of the same waitress I ordered two more drinks for us both. I needed time to think and digest this remarkable story.

"If this story is true, how can it be proved? What evidence is there? And how can I be sure that this man really was my father? What happened to him? Herr Winkler, there are so many questions, and it seems, so few answers."

"But there is the evidence! I have found it. Why do you think it has taken me so long before I dared to contact you?

If I had contacted you before I could prove any of this what would you have thought? That I was just a crackpot, hoping to gain something? No! I tell you now. I made your father a solemn promise that day to prove that all he had told me was true and to contact his wife and child. This man was indeed your father of that there is no possible doubt. The truth has to be at long last told to the whole world, and I have that proof."

"Evidence and proof, but what evidence and proof? How can you prove any of this? Surely as you have already said the Germans were busy destroying every incriminating document right up until the camp was liberated."

"That is perfectly true Herr Harper, but not all of the documents could be burnt in time, there were so many of them covering the twelve years of the camp's existence, and from the documents that have survived all of these many years, I discovered them again. All hidden away and forgotten about in the museum archives. I found them at Dachau and in the old Gestapo headquarters in Berlin where they lay undisturbed and forgotten about since the war ended. The most spectacular find was hidden in the deep vaults of the Gestapo headquarters in Prinz Albrecht Strasse; these were actually marked for the personal attention of Reich Fuhrer Himmler, head of the SS. These alone confirmed in great detail every word your father had told me.

"You must remember that the Nazis were fanatical about recording everything but could not hope to destroy all of the files they had accumulated through the war. It was these very same files that I discovered, and they revealed everything. Hitler's assassination, how the SS kept the assassination secret, and even how they duped the German

High Command so that Himmler's war for world supremacy would carry on.

"For many years I debated with myself that if his story were true it would have many repercussions. I had so many doubts as to what to do, but curiosity and the overpowering need to know became too much for me. I decided to take it upon myself to investigate the archives at Dachau and prove, or disprove it all. And history? It will have to be written again. The bodies of Hitler and Eva Braun discovered partly burnt outside the bunker by the Russians could now be finally proved not to have been that of Adolf Hitler. Did the Russians know the truth but had suppressed it from the world? If so, for what possible reason? But the evidence is all there my young friend, I know. I have the original documents and statements from witnesses to prove it all."

"But if Hitler was killed by my father how do you account for him being seen by the whole world during the course of the war? He controlled the war until the very end. And how exactly did my father die? You claim to have had this incredible conversation with him, but how do I know that?" I was getting tired and frustrated now. I wanted to know more, there were so many unanswered questions and Herr Winkler had all of the answers. My tiredness and anxiety must have shown plainly on my face.

"That is enough for today my young friend, you must be tired after your trip, and now need a bit of time for you to digest everything. Tomorrow we will go to Dachau, for I know you will never believe me unless you see Dachau for yourself and understand what a terrible place it was. With your approval I will reserve a table for us both this evening in the restaurant where we can both relax and get to know each other better, but no more talk of your father, the war or Dachau tonight Herr Harper. Tomorrow I will tell you everything, please save your questions for then, it will be easier for me to answer them as I disclose the facts to you. Ernst will collect us both in the morning at 10.00 sharp."

The following morning Ernst collected us from the hotel promptly at 10.00 after we had both met in the hotel restaurant and had eaten a good breakfast with ample cups of coffee to wash it all down. I felt that I would need my nerves today, it isn't everyday that you find out after more than forty years how your father died and under what circumstances. I had mixed feelings about going to the place where he spent the last years of his life and where he finally died, but go I must. My mother and I would never be able to find peace if I faltered now, finally so near to the truth.

So with that resolve in my heart we set off into the mid morning traffic. Ernst proved to be an excellent driver as he safely weaved his way through the traffic, speeding away from the city centre along Dachauer Strasse and into the countryside. Crossing over the E52 and through the town of Karlsfeld we travelled, Dachau coming ever nearer at each passing minute; through Rothschwaige now and a road sign giving directions to Dachau Concentration Camp, a few more minutes and I saw my first signs of the evil place where my father and many thousands of others had perished.

Pulling up in the car park I was surprised to see how many people were already here. Were they tourists or had they come to pay their respects to a loved one whose last days were spent here I wondered? Ernst would not be coming with us, but would wait in the car until our return. Leading me by the arm Herr Winkler showed a pass of some kind to the official at the camp entrance, after examining it we were both ushered through without further ado, I had the distinct impression that they both knew each other and the showing of the pass was just a formality.

The camp was now a museum and place of remembrance and pilgrimage where people of all nations and religions came to pay their respects. It must have been so very different now to what it was like in May 1945. The original wooden barracks were long gone, just the foundations remaining to show of their existence, razed to the ground by the American Army after the camp was at long last cleared of all of its inmates. Just four have been reconstructed where it is now possible to walk through them to get some idea of just what the inside of the barracks would have been like.

The barrack that we walked through was just too clean and clinical, giving no genuine sense of what they were really like with hundreds upon hundreds of filthy, starved, human beings lying side by side in such a confined space that it was all but impossible to make any movement. The original buildings must have been total squalor with the living, the dying and the dead, lying along side each other on row upon row of rough wooden bunks in stacks of four reaching up into the roof. I could imagine that those on the very top bunks must have endured the heat in the summer and then in the winter, the freezing nights. There was no heating of any kind. Each prisoner had a thin blanket and if he was fortunate enough he might have been able to use a blanket from one of his dead companions. It was known for prisoners to keep the dead amongst them just to claim their paltry ration of bread, and at best, a very thin soup or gruel which, on a very good day, may include some form of meat, horse if they were really lucky, or more likely the bones and meat of one of the many rodents than grew fat on the corpses. The two lines of poplar trees were still there as they had been when this was a place of torture and death.

Outside of what was the Administration Block stands a symbolic sculpture depicting the agony and helplessness of the inmates. It resembles many individuals who appear to be calling out for help. Looking at it one can only attempt to imagine the suffering that happened here; just what one so called human being is capable of inflicting upon another. The Administration Block now houses the museum. We went inside where I couldn't help but notice that many of the photographs on display had been defaced. Those of Hitler and the Commandant along with most of the SS guards had had their faces scratched out; such is the feeling of people, even today, so many years after the war. Many Germans visit this and other camps and like other visiting nationalities ask one just question – "Why? Why did this happen?" I wondered how I would feel, knowing that a family member had died here, but then it dawned on me with a sudden jolt that my very own father did died here. I felt suddenly very dizzy and faint. Herr Winkler gently grasped my arm and led me away to a quiet area where I could sit for a while and recover from the sudden realisation of what I had only just begun to understand. This is the place where my father was locked away, probably tortured, and died. He was not even permitted to have any contact with the other prisoners. Men, women and even children all about him but not daring to even approach him, let alone try to talk to him for fear of certain death by one of the many guards who patrolled within the wire fence. The very worst sort of solitary punishment, being with other people, seeing them walk by and being so close yet so far away.

Feeling better now I felt that I wanted to see more. Herr Winkler suggested that I might want to come back later as we were now moving onto what many people regard as a particularly emotional area, declining his kind thought and suggestion I slowly walked to the gas chambers with Herr Winkler still supporting my arm. Nobody walks quickly here; it is a sign of respect for the tens of thousands that died on the very spot where we tread today. The smell of gas still hangs in the air. The ovens in which countless thousands of bodies were disposed of brought a shudder to my spine. How could one nation and its people have possibly done such a terrible thing to other human beings? I noticed a plaque near to one of the ovens which gave the name of a young female SOE agent who tragically met her end here. Looking at her beautiful face and reading about her brought a lump into my throat and tears welled up in my eyes.

But there was now at least hope in this place of death. At the end of the main avenue there are four chapels, each representing the religious denomination of the prisoners who died here, each one a place of peace and commemoration to those that had perished here during those terrible years, Chapels of sanctuary where it is possible to enter and pray for the souls that once existed here. In the Roman Catholic Chapel the nuns in their white and black religious habit seem to glide everywhere adding to the tranquillity.

Herr Winkler turned and looked at me. There were tears in his eyes, rolling steadily down his cheeks. I had completely forgotten that he was here during those last terrible days; his memories of this foul place must be almost too much to bear even after all of the years that have passed and his many visits here since, the passage of time not diminishing the terrible sights that he witnessed and that I and others can only attempt to imagine.

Now it was my turn to help him. Taking hold of his arm I motioned him to a nearby seat to rest for a moment. “Herr Winkler, you are extremely brave to come back here. Please rest for a while. I can only imagine how you must feel walking amongst the ghosts of the past again.”

“I have returned here many times over the years, and every time is just as traumatic as the first. The Nations of the World must never forget places such as this. What happened here should never happen again. We must never deny that the Holocaust ever took place. General Eisenhower was very wise when he ordered photographs and films be produced to record forever what happened in these camps, because as he rightly said at the time “Some son of a bitch will deny it ever took place!” His words, not mine you understand.”

How right Eisenhower’s words would prove to be true. Even today, with the overwhelming evidence that exists there are some individuals and religions that deny the Holocaust ever happened.

“I have often wondered if I could have prevented your father’s death. Could I somehow, have hidden him? But I know deep down in my heart that that would have been impossible. I have been so deeply troubled since that terrible day. I will go to my grave knowing that I witnessed a very brave man die and I could do absolutely nothing to prevent it.”

This was another startling revelation. “You saw him die? You were there? You must tell me. How? Please Herr Winkler, you must tell me everything you know.”

“I will my friend. But please, not here. Let’s leave this terrible place and I will show you the evidence and proof that I have discovered and what happened to your father.”

He was perfectly correct of course. While I was anxious to discover more I especially needed some time to recover from what I had experienced today. Walking slowly back in total silence we retraced our footsteps. The same official who had examined Herr Winkler's pass stood at the gate, almost as if he was waiting for our return. He looked over in our direction and simply, but somehow meaningfully, nodded his head at us as if to say 'goodbye'; he would not meet Herr Winkler again; this would be his final visit.

Returning to the car Ernst was waiting for us and could see that we were both very emotionally affected by our visit and so did not speak; instead he opened the doors and allowed us to get in. Neither of us spoke during the journey, it had been a very moving experience for me to visit Dachau, and Herr Winkler was still very emotional.

Ernst dropped us back at the hotel where we both retired to our rooms to freshen up, agreeing to meet again in a few hours in the lounge. I took a long, hot, refreshing shower to try and comprehend all that had taken place today. I rang my mother to check that she was alright, telling her of my progress so far. She sounded very shaky, her voice trailing completely off at one point. Our neighbour now spoke, explaining that my mother hadn't been too well since I left earlier yesterday morning. The shock of everything was obviously now having an effect, delayed action if you like. Assuring me that she had called our doctor who would be calling that afternoon to examine her left me wondering whether it was such a good idea for me to come to Germany after all. Giving her the hotel's phone number I asked that once the doctor had been would she call me back to let me know the outcome of his visit, which she promised to do. I felt somewhat happier now that I had spoken to my mother, albeit concerned about her health, and yet knowing that she was in very good hands.

Looking back on the events of today I tried to get every thing into some sort of order and perspective. The German official at Dachau certainly knew Herr Winkler of that there was no doubt, had he helped him into getting privileged access to the archives I wondered? How many times had he visited Dachau to honour his pledge to my father? Each time must have been as difficult as the first, yet this now very old man had persisted such was his determination. Dressing quickly I locked my room, heading for the lounge and a refreshing beer.

The bar and lounge was almost empty, just two or three young couples sitting at the tables having a quiet drink and talking, and one older looking man sitting alone at a corner table. Walking over to a table near to the windows that overlooked the hotel gardens at the rear, I made myself comfortable. A pleasant young waitress saw me arrive and came over to take my order, as before, she spoke near perfect English so I didn't have to attempt to order a beer using my very poor German, much to mine, and probably her, relief. Although Herr Winkler wasn't here yet I ordered us both drinks. I couldn't but help think at what this young German girl knew of the war; were her parents or grandparents involved in it in some way?

She quickly returned with the two drinks, I decided to pluck up the courage and ask her! Her answer surprised me I must admit. All German schools teach their pupils about the two World Wars to some degree, and such is the abhorrence with which the German Nation now hold for Adolf Hitler and his Third Reich it is actually a crime punishable since the end of the Second World War by imprisonment to display Nazi symbols or publish pro-Nazi propaganda. Before I could continue our conversation Herr Winkler walked into the bar and I indicated to his beer that was on the table. My young waitress friend bade her thanks and went on to serve at another nearby table. As he walked over I could see he was carrying under his arm an old brown battered leather briefcase that appeared to be crammed with documents. Sitting down opposite me, he placed the briefcase carefully on the table between us.

Making himself comfortable he started to unbuckle the briefcase. "I believe you have a telephone call at the reception desk Herr Harper, the receptionist asked me to tell you." I wasn't expecting any calls except from our neighbour, perhaps she had some news for me. Picking up the receiver I spoke to her. It was only a brief message, I couldn't then, give any reply, but just said I expected to return home tomorrow. Slowly replacing the receiver, I stood there for a moment in silence, then slowly made my way back to Herr Winkler.

"This has all of the evidence you will ever need. Inside it are the original German records, original mind you, not copies, photographs and most importantly, a written statement made in the hand of the only surviving witness to Hitler's death. We must thank the SS for that. They had to be absolutely certain that they had the only witness safely locked away with your father in Dachau. Don't read them now, but take them back to England with you, I will tell you what is there. After you have read through them you must decide what it is you want to do with the information. I will tell you now all you need to know. The indisputable evidence is here in front of you. I have also enclosed full details of my conversation with your father, and more importantly, where his body is. Yes, I know the exact spot where he is buried. I was a witness to his execution and I am the last surviving member of the burial party." Picking up his glass he slowly drank from it, placing it back on the table.

I sat back in my seat in stunned silence. Did I really hear him say that he knew the exact spot where my father is buried? What else had Herr Winkler to disclose? We sat in silence for a moment. In the briefcase in front of me, just a few inches away, were all the answers to all of my questions. I had to try and take this all in. Making myself more comfortable in the chair I looked him in the eyes in an effort to read his mind. This old man sitting opposite me claims to know where my father's body is. What else would he divulge I asked myself? In a subdued but very serious voice he spoke again.

"I understand that this is a great deal for you to comprehend Herr Harper. I decided yesterday before I met with you that I would only give you some of the details of what I know. Now is the time for me to tell you everything, and I will, from the hours after meeting your father, to his execution by the camp SS and the reason for it, with an end to the war in sight. And I can explain how Hitler 'apparently' still maintained his control of the war and appeared in front of his people until his so called death in Berlin, although in fact, he had been dead since early in 1941. And your father's burial place, I will take you there later. After your father had finished telling me his truly remarkable story, I must confess now, that I didn't really believe him. I thought it the ramblings of a man who had been isolated for so long that he had gone completely mad.

"You, I am sure, are probably thinking exactly the same thing at this very moment about me; after all as yet I have not presented you with any proof. At first I was convinced that after being treated worse than an animal his mind had become deranged, and who could blame me for thinking such a thing? But there was something about this man, perhaps that look of defiance and hatred in his eyes that made me want to believe what he had told me was indeed true. Your father's trembling hands reached out to me and he took hold of my hands so very gently yet with a hidden inner strength. Our eyes met and it was then that he made me vow to Almighty God, that if I survived that terrible place I would seek out his wife and son and tell them the truth about his last days on this Earth. His words were so emotional, almost over powering in his belief of what he had just told me, that without any hesitation I gladly promised that I would do everything in my power to do just that. There were tears in his eyes as I promised that I would, a look came upon his face as if a huge weight had now been lifted off of his hunched shoulders, he actually seemed happy, there was the faintest of smiles on his once young looking but now aged and weathered face. His hands slowly unclasped from mine, and he slumped back into the bench almost collapsing onto the filthy floor. He seemed to be at peace, no longer caring what his fate was to be, although I'm sure that he knew that his days on this Earth were numbered.

"But did he really kill Hitler? This I found difficult to accept. I had been forced to go to many of the Nazi party rallies with the Hitler Youth since 1941, where I had seen Hitler with my very own eyes standing in front of thousands of devoted followers, speaking so fervently, rallying all 'good Germans' to the Nazi cause, so how could your father's story have any truth in it? It was then that another prisoner came over to speak to him. He too had the same red circles and the initials 'NN' on his clothing. He sat down beside your father and gently took his hand in his, they both looked at each other and tears began to well up in their eyes until they were running down their cheeks and dropping onto their grubby coats leaving streaks of liquid upon the filthy surface. It was then that two of the SS guards came storming into the barracks. Your father and this other man warned me to quickly move away before the guards found me talking to them. Reluctantly I slid away, mingling in amongst the other prisoners. When I was brave enough to look back over to the bench they had both gone, the bench was laying on its side."

I could hardly believe what Herr Winkler had just told me, it was such an incredible story. But there was a witness to my father's imprisonment. If only he could be found to prove it all, if indeed, even if he had survived Dachau and after all these years, was still alive.

Herr Winkler signalled to a man sitting at another table in the far corner of the lounge, my eyes following to where he had just raised his hand. From this table an old man arose and slowly walked towards us. He had some difficulty in walking, almost stumbling at times. At first I took little notice of him, thinking that Herr Winkler had spotted an old friend of his and was just indicating that he had seen him, but as he came nearer to us it was obvious that he intended to make himself known. Then I remembered him as being the same old gentleman who had been sitting there when I first came into the lounge. Herr Winkler slowly moved towards him and greeting him with a warm handshake, assisted him to a chair at our table. He had a similar appearance to that of Herr Winkler, obviously of some age, but much older I thought,

"Herr Harper. Please allow me introduce you to that other prisoner who had befriended your father in Dachau. Please meet Herr Sachs - Gert Sachs, a former inmate of Dachau and the last known surviving servant from Adolf Hitler's Berchtesgaden."

This brief introduction hit me solidly between the eyes! I sat there in utter amazement - speechless. Quickly gathering my wits I arose and shook him gently by the hand. I could see that this was a man who had clearly suffered a great deal during his life. His face was drawn and gaunt; the eyes, though looking bright and full of life were sunk into darkened sockets. His health was plainly very poor. I looked at Herr Winkler with a mixture of many emotions. I was puzzled and yet inquisitive, for sitting just a few feet to the side of me was probably the last man on Earth who saw my father alive.

"I have had considerable trouble trying to locate Herr Sachs," he glanced towards him with a sly but knowing smile on his face, at the same time reaching across the table and gently taking hold of his frail old hands as if to comfort him, "until just a few weeks ago I believed him to be dead and had almost given up any hope of finding him alive, when, through the post I received a letter from him in reply to a newspaper appeal that I had been running for some time in both local and national newspapers. There were times, Herr Harper, when I thought that I would never find him. He was as elusive as a shadow on a very dark night. And who could blame him? He had no idea who I was and why, after so many years, was I trying to trace him. But let Herr Sachs tell you more."

The old man shifted in his seat trying to get more comfortable, turning towards me, and in a low, quivering voice he began to speak, and like Herr Winkler, in excellent English. "Everything Herr Winkler has told you is perfectly true. I know, because I was there at Berchtesgaden and later at Dachau and saw it all. My name is Gert Sachs and I was employed as a servant on Hitler's domestic staff." He hesitated for a moment and then continued.

"I had been employed there from shortly after Hitler had completed the substantial building improvements which he embarked upon after acquiring the old villa Haus Wachenfeld in June of 1936. I was declared unfit for military service as I have a collapsed lung from a childhood illness. Wishing to serve my Fuhrer in some way - in those far off days I truly believed Adolf Hitler to be Germany's saviour - I applied for the post and was accepted; I believe that Hitler, being informed of my desire to serve the Fatherland in some way, had agreed to my employment. I worked hard and was promoted into a position of trust. One of my many responsibilities was to ensure that all of the rooms within the villa were cleared of crockery and left tidy after Hitler had retired to his conference room to meet with his military leaders, you know Goering and the like, although Goering wasn't actually present on that particular night."

I interrupted at this point. "That particular night, what does that mean?" "Patience my young friend, Herr Sachs will explain all to you." It was Herr Winkler speaking.

"I had just started on my rounds that evening, I think I was a bit late that night for some reason, when it was with some surprise that just as I was leaving one of the rooms I noticed a door being opened at the other end. I found this surprising, as I knew that apart from myself there shouldn't have been anybody else in that part of the villa, Hitler was having a meeting with some General or other in his conference room, so I decided to see who it could possibly be. Who knows, it could have been 'fatso' Hermann Goering!" He gave a chuckle at this point. "With my door slightly ajar I had a clear view of the opposite door, and to my amazement this scruffily dressed man appeared with a gun in his hand. My first instinct was to raise the alarm, but for some reason I didn't utter a word. Where had he come from? How did he get past our guard on the steps?

"I watched as he moved silently about the room, picking up photographs of Hitler and his mistress Eva Braun and replacing them carefully. I couldn't make out who he could be or what he was after. He was wearing a long battered old overcoat and those leather boots that Bavarian farmers wear. As he lent over to look at something his overcoat opened and I could see that underneath he was wearing a military uniform. I recognised the 'wings' on the tunic and immediately guessed that this man was an escaping British airman. So what was I to do? I did nothing! Why? To this day I do not know the answer to that question even though I have asked myself a thousand times. He replaced the photographs and made his way back the same way that he had entered the room, carefully and silently closing the door behind him. I decided that I must follow and find out what he was doing here.

"I very silently crept after him but once I was outside on the terrace I could not see him anywhere, he had vanished into thin air. Was I dreaming I asked myself? It was then that I could hear Hitler's voice shouting and screaming from his conference room. I knew that it could not be because this man had been discovered as there was no way into the conference room from the terrace unless the panoramic windows were open, and I knew that they were closed as that particular night it was very cold and Hitler had given strict instructions that all external doors and windows were to be closed to keep the cold night air out. He, Hitler that is, must have been arguing with the officer whom he was talking to.

"Shortly after I could hear the windows being opened - they drop down below the terrace you know, very clever - and I watched as Hitler strode out, obviously in a rage. He held his hands clenched behind his back and he stamped his feet to show his bad temper and contempt, no doubt for the officer who had either disagreed with him or who had suggested something else. Then I saw this man again as he stepped from the shadows just beside the window where he had obviously been hiding.

"Hitler by this time had reached the low wall and was leaning forward on it, probably admiring his native Austria in the moonlight reflecting from the far off mountain peaks. Then this man slowly and silently crept up behind him. I saw him raise the pistol to Hitler's head and he fired, three times. Hitler fell to the ground; his head was almost blown apart by the impact of the bullets. The man then raised the pistol again, but this time to his own head. I could hear the firing pin clicking as it struck on an empty chamber, not once but about three times. His hand dropped like a heavy weight to his side and he collapsed onto the terrace beside Hitler's body.

"By now the whole villa was alert after the gunshots were heard and guards were running everywhere not knowing where the shots had come from. I ran back into the servants' quarters before I was discovered. I did not want to become involved in what I had just witnessed. I feared for my own life. Unfortunately another servant informed the SS the following day. It seems he had wanted me for something and had gone to my room where I should have been. He was an out and out Nazi, where as I just wanted an easy, comfortable job and was never interested in politics. I was arrested and taken to the Gestapo headquarters in Berlin where I was, how shall I put it, 'persuaded' to confess all. I was forced to write a statement in my own hand, as to what this man had done. I was secretly hoping that in doing so my life would be spared and I would receive only a light prison sentence in a civilian jail.

"But no! None of that! I was classified as a 'Nacht und Nebel' prisoner as was your father, condemned to be lost forever within the Third Reich. Nobody would ever know who we are, and we would cease to exist except in highly classified records kept only by the Himmler and his SS, filed away and forgotten, that is until Herr Winkler here came along.

"So that is why I was sent to Dachau with Andrew. Please, I hope that it is correct for me to call your father by his Christian name, you see, we became firm friends in Dachau. Two of a kind as it were. Shunned by the other prisoners we would have gone completely mad if we hadn't stuck together. We were both imprisoned there since that day knowing that the SS would never permit us to leave - not alive anyway.

"By 1945 the SS knew the war was lost and wanted to 'dispose' of the living evidence to Hitler's death. But Himmler would not sign our death warrants, he wanted us both to suffer for as long as possible, probably hoping that we would die of 'natural' causes eventually."

He paused for a breath. He was shaking and still very emotional by what he had just said even though many years had passed. Herr Winkler called for a glass of water for him.

Seeing that the old man could not carry on Herr Winkler continued with the rest of the story.

"And so it was Herr Harper, that two SS guards came into the barracks and took them both away and they were placed in separate cells over night. Your father was taken out very early the following morning and an SS Death Squad shot him to death. For some still unknown reason Herr Sachs was not executed, but evaded the SS Death Squad until the American Army liberated the camp the following day.

"He was ordered by the regular German Army camp guards, not the SS, who by now had realised that the Americans were close by and who had now deserted their posts and vanished in a vain attempt to evade justice, to bury your father in secret fearing that they would now be held responsible for his death. Just one day later the American 42nd Division of the 7th Army liberated the camp, just one day! If only the Americans could have arrived that day earlier your father may have been saved from execution."

So now I knew how and why my father had died. Not when his Lancaster was shot down in 1941, but later at the very place we had visited earlier today. I could have trodden in his very footsteps as I walked around the camp. I glanced at Herr Sachs who was obviously emotionally exhausted. To recount his memories at his age and state of health was plainly very telling on him. He just sat there, his eyes at some distant place and in a different era, slowly, so slowly, sipping from the glass of water.

"I realise this is very difficult for you, but please continue if you are able to Herr Winkler. You said you know where my father is buried? Is it close by? You must take me there as soon as is possible. This has been my quest, to find out what happened to my father, and now, thanks to you and

Herr Sachs, to find him at long last."

"Yes, I will take you there, but Herr Sachs will not come with us. As you can see he would find the experience just too painful to bear. Until I saw him this evening I wasn't sure if he would really be here to tell you in his own words. He has had to endure a lot over the years since the war ended. At one time he was admitted into a special hospital for expert treatment to help him come to terms with everything. Newspapers hounded him, not because of your father of course, they had no idea about that thank God, but because he was on Adolf Hitler's staff, pestering him for stories and other bits of information to help sell their newspapers. They didn't make life very easy for him. Eventually he took on a new name and life for himself. He married and has raised a son and daughter. They alone persuaded him to come today. Look across there to the other table and you will see them there waiting to take care of their father and safely see him home."

I looked across the lounge and true enough, a man and a woman, no older than myself, was sitting at another table. I wondered if they knew who I was earlier as I passed their table not realising who they were. They acknowledge me with a nod of their heads. Both of their faces had an apologetic expression, tinged with a look of guilt for what had occurred all of those years ago. They couldn't be held responsible for the past. I nodded back and smiled at them both. If they hadn't persuaded their father to come today the whole outcome of my trip would have been totally different. Strange I thought. Their father luckily survived Dachau, but mine didn't. I wondered how different everything would have been if my father had survived as well, to return to England safely, to his wife, and his newborn son. To survive the war and settle back into civilian life, how different would I be now? I certainly wouldn't be sitting here with Herr Winkler. And what of him? He has spent the best part of his life fulfilling his promise to my father. What might he have achieved? We will never know. All I do know is that there is no way that I can ever fully express my thanks to him for what he has done.

Herr Winkler spoke and awoke me from my thoughts of what might have been. "Herr Harper, I know the exact location, but I need to answer your other questions before I take you. You see, when I take you to your father's resting place, it will be for me the end of many years research, a final closure for me if you like. But for you I feel that it will be just the beginning. You will have all the proof you need to tell the rest of the world - if you should choose - the truth surrounding Hitler's death. That will become your task in life. There are still people - and Nations - that would prefer that the truth is never known. The Russians who during the Cold War period, kept so much hidden from the Western Powers regarding their discovery of Hitler's and Eva Braun's burnt bodies. Neo Nazi groups who claim and believe that 'their Fuhrer' really escaped at the last moment before Berlin fell to the Russians, and would like to see the resurrection of Nazism and all it stands for. Your struggle is now only just beginning my friend. I only hope that with time you and your mother will find closure, knowing what really happened on that eventful day so many years ago."

His words sounded to me like a challenge, daring me to tell the whole world the truth regardless of the possible consequences it might have. It was a challenge! He wanted the whole world to know and was, in his own way, pleading with me to tell it and end the myth that Hitler escaped the

Allies and survived to live in hiding, possibly in South America, protected by a network of ex-Nazis.

"Since my mother and I received your letter I had hung onto the hope that I could find his body and bring it back to England so that my mother can lie alongside him when she passes away. You see, she was so very frail and I'm afraid your letter was just too much for her. I had already spoken on the phone earlier to a friend who was looking after her whilst I was away. In the space of an hour she called me back, that was the message you gave me about the telephone call at the reception desk. She rang to tell me that she had suffered a severe heart attack and had died a few minutes earlier. My mother will never know the truth now, but her suffering at the loss of her husband over these last, long years will not torment her anymore. She is at last, at peace. There is no blame on yourself Herr Winkler, my mother had been in very poor health for some time."

A look of shock and grief showed in his face. I could see that Herr Sachs was also terribly upset, tears appearing in his eyes. The news of my mother's sudden death was completely unexpected by either of them.

"I am so sorry Herr Harper. Doubly sorry that your mother is dead, and also because she will never know what a very brave man her husband was. Please excuse me for a moment." He rose from his seat and walked over to the bar where Ernst had been waiting in case we should need his services again today. A few words were exchanged between them, Ernst looked over towards me, nodded his head, and then left.

"I have informed Ernst that we will not need him until early tomorrow morning when he will take us to where your father is buried. But now to tell you what you need to know about how your father was executed. I will not give you every detail, you can find whatever else you need to know in here." Putting his hand on top of the thick, well-worn briefcase he slowly slid it across the table to me. Looking me in the eyes he conveyed a silent message to me - take great care of it and believe what you find within its pages.

He continued. "Early the next day I witnessed four SS men drag your father out of the compound and away to an isolated barrack in another part of the camp. Herr Sachs was not with him although he had been taken with your father the day before. Before I could move away I was grabbed by another SS guard and together with another prisoner, we were ordered to prepare a grave in the woods just outside of the camp. Two SS officers and two soldiers escorted us by truck to the forest where we were forced to dig a grave for one body. Our first thoughts were that we were going to dig our own graves but when we were ordered to dig only one we were greatly relieved, at least we might survive to see our eventual liberation which must surely come soon, we could clearly hear the artillery fire coming closer each day.

"After a few hours of hard digging; the ground was very rocky which made it extremely hard work and there were so many heavy rocks to move away, we eventually had dug deep enough. The two SS officers who had been standing nearby talking and smoking inspected the grave and grunted their satisfaction. We were then driven back to the camp and frog marched to an area where executions by firing squad were carried out. At first we both believed we were to die now, but why not just shoot us in the forest and leave our bodies to rot? Shouting from the direction of the barracks made us turn to see what was happening. It was your father being dragged along by two burly guards, this was the last time I saw your father alive. He was dragged from the building and made to stand in front of a bullet riddled brick wall. From his appearance he had obviously been severely beaten, his face was bruised and swollen, and blood had congealed on a stubbly growth of beard. He could hardly walk, every now again he would stumble to the ground to be roughly hauled to his feet by the guards. They tied him roughly to one of the many posts and they offered him a blindfold, which he refused, preferring to look at his executioners straight into their eyes. We could now see the accompanying firing squad being assembled. Ten riflemen to shoot one prisoner. They were lined up into two rows of five, the front row knelt, the rear row standing, an officer gave the order to load their rifles and ten rifle bolts clicked in unison, the same officer gave the order to take aim and then the order to fire was given, ten rifle bullets speeding to your father's heart, it was all over in a matter of a few seconds. He was dead, his now lifeless body slumping down, only the rope supporting him in place on the post. It was all over so very quickly.

"One of the SS officers approached your father, removed his Lugar pistol from its holster, took aim at his head and fired a single bullet into his brain. It was over. The firing squad was then stood to attention, their rifles slung over their shoulders and dismissed, marching away with no apparent feelings or emotions as to what they had just carried out. To them it was just another execution, one of hundreds if not thousands they had carried out over the years."

At this point Herr Winkler appeared to almost break down, the memory and emotions of that day coming back as real as if he was living it all over again. But quickly recovering and again taking control of his emotions, he continued.

"The two of us were forced to cut him down and then place his body into a very rough cloth sack, the sack was prominently marked with a similar red circle and 'NN' to that on his clothes. It was into this sack that we placed your father's limp and bloodied body. We then lifted him onto an old wooden handcart for removal to a nearby waiting army truck. His death was to be kept so secret that the SS did not want to risk using any other prisoners to push the cart for fear that they would discover what had just taken place. Neither of us didn't expect to be alive after the burial, we believed the SS would eliminate all witnesses, more so if the SS knew that I now had knowledge of your father's and Gert Sachs's story. If they had any idea of what I knew I would not be here now telling you. We were under the glare of an SS officer and guard all of the time. We daren't even look up from the ground for fear that they would kill us both there and then.

"The same army truck that had taken us to the wood to prepare the grave appeared from close by, and, with the tail gate lowered, we lifted your father's body into the back of it sliding him along the floor between two rows of wooden seats which ran alongside both sides of the truck. SS guards, armed to the teeth, were all around, making certain that no prying eyes were witnessing what was happening. Any prisoners that did get too close were clubbed with rifle butts; some fell unconscious to the ground whilst others scurried for the shelter of their barracks. We were then ordered into the back of the truck with his body, several well aimed kicks from their boots hurried us both along, a tarpaulin sheet was dropped down at the back so that there was no possibility of any uninvited and curious eyes seeing inside. We were driven out of the gates and back along the same route to the lonely grave in the wood, all the time with guards covering us both with their rifles and automatic pistols.

"These animals of soldiers showed no respect at all for the dead. All the way to the woods they rested their jack-booted legs on your father's body. How I wish I could have said or done something, but there was no point, I would have been beaten or shot for my insolence and they would still have continued in their barbaric way.

"Arriving finally at the woods we carried him to the graveside. Here we lowered him into the ground and we covered him with soil and then piled some of the rocks on top to prevent wild animals from digging down into the now soft earth in an attempt to get at the body. The grave was not marked in any way, not even a cross was placed upon it. The SS had all been drinking freely and were without doubt, quite intoxicated which might explain why we too, weren't shot on the spot.

"We were ordered back into the truck again with the help of a well-aimed rifle butt and jackboot. In his drunken stupor one guard mistimed his kick at me and promptly fell onto his face at which the other guards roared with laughter. This clearly angered him and so he kicked us both even more until he had taken out his vengeance on us both.

"They must also have been very sure of themselves and confident that they would get away with what they had just committed, because after we returned to the camp we were amazingly allowed to return to our barracks and mix freely with the other prisoners. Perhaps because of the amount of schnapps' or wine that they had consumed they had overlooked the two of us. No doubt if they had been sober we would both be singled out for execution, after all, we had witnessed everything.

"We moved away as quickly as we were able before they changed their minds and hid ourselves away amongst the other inmates, not daring to show ourselves in fear that they would come searching for us later. Nobody asked us what had happened to us or where we had been, although several saw us both get into the truck and drive off, such was the fear that they would be singled out for 'special treatment' for asking too many questions. With rescue coming ever closer day by day nobody wanted to put his life at risk. Sadly my companion was later 'selected' for the gas chambers and herded away with so many others. Somehow I was fortunate enough to survive, hiding wherever I could until the Americans arrived the next day and freed us all. The SS had deserted the camp several hours before their arrival as had most of the guards. Those that remained were either too drunk to run or put themselves at the mercy of the Americans, mercy indeed, what mercy did these animals show us? We did hear rumours that some of the American troops shot several out of hand in their rage and anger when they found the piles of dead bodies. I for one prayed that they did."

Herr Winkler released an audible sigh of relief. By telling me his story he had, after all of these years, managed to release a great weight from his now, old shoulders. We sat there in silence for a moment. So much to take in and comprehend. The German military was well aware that the war was lost, why did they have to carry on murdering? I at last knew the full story of my father's terrible existence; for that is what it really was - an existence, and how he had met his death. "But Herr Winkler, didn't you report all of this to the American liberators?"

"Yes, of course I did, but with all of the confusion and urgency to care for the survivors and burying the dead before cholera and other diseases spread throughout the camp I made a brief statement and it was put to one side to be investigated later by the War Crimes Investigators and the Comite' International de Dachau at a later date. But by the time any investigations for war crimes had begun I had been repatriated and the war was over, so it was either forgotten about or lost in a tangle of, how do you say, red tape? The hunt was on for Hitler and other leaders of the Third Reich, other camps had been liberated and the Commandants arrested, all had to be investigated and proof discovered to prosecute these people to bring them to justice. The Allied Powers had just too many members of the Nazi hierarchy to locate, arrest and investigate the crimes they committed. It was because of this lack of interest on their part when they had other issues to pursue that I decided to prove what I knew to be true.

"So my own investigations began, but the new German authorities wanted a closure to what happened at Dachau and other concentration camps, and were not, to say the least, at all sympathetic towards me. And after all, who could blame them? Hitler assassinated by a shot down English bomber pilot? Absolutely ridiculous! Hadn't the Russians found his burnt body outside of the bunker together with his wife Eva Braun? And the Cold War had started, did the Western Powers want to provoke the mighty Soviet Union by saying they were wrong? No my friend, it was all politics! The time was to rebuild Europe, and for Germany, a divided Germany remember, to forge new, lasting bonds of international friendship and trust with her neighbours."

I pondered on this for a moment. Of course he was perfectly correct in what he was saying, after all, I originally found it difficult to believe him so why should the Allied occupying powers and the new German Government. But how did the SS manage to fool the German High Command and German public for so many years? Hitler was seen by tens of thousands, including Herr Winkler, giving speeches and rallying the faithful. And the Armed forces, even they believed that their Fuhrer was still alive and conducting the war, how could they have been duped?

As if being able to read my inner most thoughts Herr Winkler answered them. "As for Hitler being able to apparently still be alive Herr Harper, that is so simple. The SS were determined that the war should continue to the bitter end, win or loose. So what did they do? They found a double! Some one who could imitate Hitler so cleverly that even the High Command would be fooled. And just such a person was already in custody in Dachau. Dieter Bosch had already been arrested before the war had started for impersonating the Fuhrer in a Berlin nightclub frequented by many members of the Nazi party. He was so good that many people in the audience were convinced that they were actually watching Hitler. Unfortunately for him, as Hitler became much more powerful and he became Germany's Chancellor, Dieter Bosch was arrested on stage one night and dragged away by the 'Brown Shirts' and Hitler Youth. His act was considered to be a great insult to the Fuhrer and although he had been kept under constant surveillance, was not arrested until Hitler's cronies were sure that he could be prosecuted. Even his family was arrested on some trumped up charge.

"Bosch was taken into custody by the SS and after a brief trial, sent to Dachau. I knew that the German's were fanatical about keeping accurate records, so with the little information that I had it didn't take me too long for his arrest and trial records to be located. Here was the perfect double! The SS were overjoyed that they had the perfect impersonator already in their hands. Bosch was made a simple offer, agree to impersonate the Fuhrer or face the immediate liquidation of himself and all of his family who were also now interned in Dachau. Play the part as he was instructed and he and his family would be well provided for. He would be relatively 'free', although under constant observation with at least four SS officers accompanying him whenever he was in the public's eye. As for his family, they were spirited away to a secure location and put under house arrest. There would be no contact with them. What would any prisoner have said? Of course he agreed to take over the role of Adolf Hitler, under the circumstances what entertainer or actor wouldn't have agreed to stand before thousands of devout Nazis at rallies and take on the role of their beloved Fuhrer.

"There were many failed attempts on Hitler's, or as we now know, on Herr Bosch's life. The most publicised being the 'Wolf's Lair' plot of 1944, when the whole scheme could so easily have been discovered but for the fact that our impersonator survived to continue in the role of Germany's saviour. It had already been thought by several high-ranking officers in the German High Command that their Fuhrer was in fact an impersonator but they could not or dare not voice their suspicions. But if they could eliminate him then they could confidently take control of all of the Armed Forces, sue for peace, and throw themselves on the mercy of the Allied Powers. Was it just a stroke of luck that the location of the conference was moved, or was Himmler and his SS aware that their deception had been discovered? At a stroke they were able to eliminate all opposition and create the myth that Adolf Hitler was invincible and God was on the German people's side. The war would continue un-abated until Germany was in ruins. "

This was amazing. We had used a similar ploy during the war when an actor and serving member of the British Army, Clifton Webb, was persuaded to impersonate Field Marshal Montgomery. Clifton Webb's deception lasted for a few months only, but nonetheless, came under the very same close scrutiny that Dieter Bosch had to face.

"So from 1941 Herr Harper, the Third Reich and the German High Command was in reality, being 'controlled' by Dieter Bosch, albeit his every word and action was on the orders of Himmler and the SS. This will explain why many of the military decisions made by 'Hitler' were at the least strange. The real Adolf Hitler was a very good tactician, just look at the success of the German armed forces up until then.

"Blitzkrieg, a completely new concept of conducting a war. No more mile upon mile of trenches and front lines as in the First World War leading to a stalemate, but a lightening war where mobility and shock tactics ruled supreme. But once Himmler and his SS took control they were simply not up to the task of running the war as Hitler had been.

"'Operation Barbarossa', would the genuine Hitler have really invaded the Soviet Union to start a war on two fronts? Could this not have been the very argument that your father overheard at Berchtesgaden when Hitler - the genuine Hitler - was very likely over ruling the high ranking

Wermacht officer, and didn't want to start a war on two fronts? There was after all, a signed non-aggression pact between the Soviet Union and Germany. No, my friend, before the invasion of Russia could take place, Hitler knew that England must first be neutralised either by invasion and occupation or by an end to hostilities by mutual agreement - remember that England stood alone for three years until the vast resources of the United States of America were activated after the Japanese attack on Pearl Harbor on December 7th 1941.

"After the Soviet army rallied and commenced their offensive, his, that is Herr Bosch and the SS, ordered that no German forces were to retreat under any circumstances. Many were surrounded by the Russians and annihilated. No my friend. If your father had not killed Hitler the war could have turned out so differently. Imagine if the real Hitler had not been killed in 1941 and had unleashed his Tiger tanks when the Allies landed in Normandy, they would have pushed the Allied landing forces back into the English Channel, as it was Himmler had his impostor order them to be held back until it was too late and the Allies secured a firm foothold from the five invasion beachheads.

"But for your father's gallant action, the war could have turned out so very differently - even lost, and that really doesn't bear thinking about."

"But the bodies of Hitler and Eva Braun burned beyond recognition at the bunker. Did that really happen?"

"Oh yes. Himmler and the SS wanted the legacy of the Third Reich and Hitler to continue. They really believed that there would be an uprising by the German people at some time in the future to restore the Nazi party to power, and to that end the German nation should never know of their deception. So Dieter Bosch and Eva Braun had to be murdered by the SS. They did not commit suicide but were both shot in the bunker after being drugged, and the world was led to believe that they decided that they would never be taken alive and humiliated by the Russians, but had died for the Fatherland. But the Russians and Josef Stalin un-be-knowing actually played into the hands of the SS and many die hard Nazis by not giving the Allied Powers and Western nations access to the remains where proper forensic tests could have proved that this supposed body of Adolf Hitler was, as yet, an unknown corpse."

Nothing this man can tell me now will ever shock or amaze me! This was an incredible story, and the proof lay just a few inches away in front of me in a grubby old briefcase. I truly did not know what to say.

"A truly incredible story Herr Winkler, almost unbelievable. But did the Russians really believe that they had found the burnt remains of Hitler and Eva Braun?"

"At first yes, but checking the dental records of Hitler against those on the remains they discovered they did not match. Hitler's dental records showed that he had had extensive dental repair work carried out some years earlier, when most of his teeth were replaced. The corpse however, had a near perfect set of teeth. So they knew that Hitler had escaped, or so they thought. They had no idea that a double had been used up to the very end of the war. They didn't have access to the records and files that the American Army had discovered, and those that I later re-discovered at Dachau. The Russians were sure that it was Eva Braun's body, but what do they tell their Allies about Hitler? After all, they were the first into the capital of the Third Reich. Letting a prize like Hitler out of their grasp would do the

Russians no good at all, so they kept quiet and let the rest of the world believe he was dead. Imagine what a newly formed neo-Nazi party would make of it. They would believe that the Fuhrer was still alive and living in South America. It could have started a third world war. No my friend, the Russians were correct in their decision. As far as the world was concerned Adolf Hitler and his Third Reich were long dead and buried never to rise again!"

All that Herr Winkler said made perfect sense of course. It was getting very late. The bar was deserted and we had sat here for what seemed an eternity, and now everything seemed much clearer. My father was a true hero and should be recognised as such.

"But that is enough for now. It is very late and tomorrow we have an early start. I have arranged for Ernst to collect us at 10.00 again. Tomorrow we go to find your father's grave."

With these last words echoing in my head we retired for the night. I found sleep impossible, much like a child who is going on a trip in the morning and couldn't sleep through anticipation of what the coming day would bring. As Herr Winkler approached the final hours of his quest, I knew that mine was just beginning.

Chapter 7

Search and Discovery

Promptly as arranged at 10.00 Ernst arrived at the hotel to pick us up. Herr Winkler was already waiting for me in the lobby. Greeting me he motioned towards the waiting car, its engine still running on the hotel's forecourt. This was the day at last. I was to be taken to my father's grave. I felt very nervous and somewhat apprehensive. I did not know what to expect or how I would react, but with a reassuring smile from Herr Winkler and Ernst I became much calmer. I knew I was in good hands, for this, the final part of my journey, and yet the beginning of another.

We headed off in the early morning traffic in the direction of Dachau, along the same roads we had taken before. None of us spoke, sitting there in silence. Ernst even had his radio turned off as if in respect for our journey and where we were going. It was as if we were going to a funeral or some other solemn occasion, which indeed we were. Shortly before arriving at the entrance to Dachau Ernst turned off of the main road and drove along a very minor road heading towards some distant hills. Looking over I could clearly see the barbed wire fence and the guard towers that surrounded the camp.

This road was barely paved and obviously not used a great deal, except perhaps, by the local farmers whose fields of ripening wheat or corn, the wind gently swaying the heads to and fro, were on either side. The road was made up of mainly large flat stones with a section or two of tarmac here and there, probably I thought, all that was left of the original surface laid down many years ago. Where farm traffic and weather had worn and eroded the tarmac away stones were used to fill in the many pot-holes. Driving slowly now, as the road became even more pot-holed and rougher it suddenly came to an end and finally disappeared to become no more than a grassy trackway through the surrounding wild flowers and weeds as we passed the last of the cornfields. As we went further along the overgrowth at the edge of the track became much thicker; hawthorn bushes, their flowers in full bloom, scraping along the side of the car, reaching out as if to greet us. Eventually these gave way to much denser countryside, the track now heading deeper into a thickly wooded pine forest. With the windows open the smell of the pines flowed into my nostrils, the sudden coolness from the shade of the tall trees was very welcome after the hot drive. It was difficult to imagine that just a few miles from this peaceful wood there stood a place of such immense evil.

We had to stop now; an old heavy wooden gate barred our way. Ernst left the car and walked over to the gate to lift it clear of the ground, managing to open it enough for us to drive through. A mile or so further on and Ernst turned off going ever deeper into the forest. He appeared to be following tracks made by several other vehicles that seemed to point the way through the flattened and crushed grass. We must have been slowly driving for about twenty minutes when Ernst finally pulled over into a clearing in the woods.

I was surprised to see that there were two other cars parked here already, it must have been these vehicles that had marked the way for us. A reception committee? I was puzzled, but should have realised that Herr Winkler had arranged all this in advance. Pulling up alongside the other vehicles we stepped out of the car.

Looking around my first impression was how peaceful it was. Birds were singing in the tall trees, and the smell of the pines in the cool air was almost overwhelming. What a stark contrast to what happened here over 40 years ago. So this was the moment. Herr Winkler invited me to follow him, walking off along a freshly trodden path, into the forest. Ernst stayed behind with the cars having excused himself from coming any further with us. We went even deeper amongst the pines until we came to a small open area where several other men were waiting. I spotted a wooden coffin on trestles placed to one side. Involuntary I took a deep breath and swallowed in an attempt to moisten my throat that was now very dry with nervousness and anticipation. My body began to shake and the hairs on the back of my neck stood up, I must control my emotions, now was not the time to be overcome by what lay ahead.

“Herr Harper. May I introduce Herr Wilkinson and Herr Braun? They are here at my request to help you in you quest. Herr Wilkinson is a member of your British War Graves Commission and Herr Braun is a registered exhumer of war graves employed by the German Federal Government. The other two gentlemen will exhume your father’s grave following our instructions, and will then remove his body and place it in this coffin.”

They all greeted me warmly, but with, I felt, great respect. I was not expecting anything like this. Herr Winkler was certainly full of surprises.

"Herr Harper. With your permission, I will now try and locate your father's grave. It has been many years since I have been here, but I would never forget just where to look. You see, after I was freed from the camp in 1945 I returned here and placed upon the grave a cairn of stones and wooden cross with your father's name cut into it. I also cut into some of the trees several clear markers using an axe, to make sure that I could find the correct location. I had to be certain that if this day ever came I would know exactly where to look. And now that day has at long last arrived."

He indicated to the two other men who picked up two spades. Examining each of the surrounding trees carefully in turn, he found the same axe cuts in the bark that he had left all of those years ago. They were now healed, but plainly visible as old scars at about eye level. Moving to a central point that appeared to be within an area formed by a triangle of the three trees he had now found with his cut marks, he excitedly started to trample down the undergrowth with the assistance of the two gravediggers. Standing now in quite a large area he frantically scanned the ground, looking for the remains of the cairn of stones and cross, if it survived, that marked my father's resting place. Calling to the two men he told them to look for a pile of large rocks and for signs of the wooden cross; these stones were probably the very same ones he had removed when he dug my father's grave with Herr Sachs. Cutting back the thick undergrowth further they searched for the pile of stones he had left here over 40 years ago. I prayed to God above that they would still be here and had not collapsed to be swallowed up by years of vegetation growing over them hiding them forever.

One of the gravediggers called out excitedly, pointing to what looked like no more than a bump in amongst the ferns and grass. Herr Winkler moved over to examine their find, reaching down he carefully lifted up what remained of the wooden cross, now fallen to the ground and almost rotted away. "Here, dig here." he shouted excitedly. "Herr Harper, this is your father's grave."

I made my way closer to see, and sure enough, there was a neat pile of stones covered with many years growth of moss, just as he had left them all of those years ago. The two men removed the heavy stones, carefully putting them to one side, treating them as if they were religious symbols, which, in a way, they were.

"You will need to dig down to about one metre, then take great care, for the body will be very close." Herr Winkler was very precise in his instructions. Looking at him now I needn't have worried about showing my emotions today. He was plainly very upset; his body seemed to be shaking as if he was very cold, his voice although very assertive, was, I thought, on the brink of faltering. He was re-living the past, I had no doubt of that. Tears were beginning to swell up in his old eyes as he remembered ever more clearly now the events of long ago. I moved over to him. I could not bear to see him suffer like this. Taking his hand in mine he looked at me and nodded in acknowledgement, a brief smile showed in his face before he looked away at the two men to make sure that all was well.

The two men acknowledged what he had said and commenced to dig. I looked again at Herr Winkler. I owed so much to this man, how could I ever repay him? He had spent many years of his life researching and finding the evidence he needed to prove my father's story. He could have just as easily forgotten about it and never mention it to anybody, but he hadn't. What a debt of gratitude I owed him.

The two men continued digging, getting deeper now into the rich, dark soil. They knew exactly how large a hole to excavate. There were no rocks to be found, they had already been dug out years ago. One of the men stopped digging and instructed the other to do the same. Kneeling down he examined something within the earth just below the surface where they had now reached. "Herr Winkler! We have found bones!"

Those few words were electrifying. The two men digging stepped away from where the bones were exposed. Yes, clearly visible were the bones of my father. Taking great care now, and putting to one side the spades, the men continued using hand trowels, carefully exposing more remains. Some of the original sackcloth used to carry his body after the execution remained attached to the bones as were shreds of the striped prison clothing. One by one the bones were very gently removed and placed with dignity into the silk lined coffin. Looking at his remains I broke down in tears, not being able to control my emotions any longer. Everyone else had moved silently away to allow me time to reflect. They were standing at a distance to leave me alone in my moment of mixed grief and happiness. Grief because of how my father had died and happiness because, now, at long last, we were reunited and he could be re-buried in consecrated ground. I was determined to take his body back to England to be buried alongside his wife, my mother where they would be re-united, together again as they should be.

Herr Winkler came to my side and placed his arm around my shoulders. He too was overcome and was openly crying. What was he thinking? The memories of my father and Dachau must now all be flooding back to him, like a hellish nightmare from his past. Now, perhaps, he could put his ghosts to rest at long last.

Moving away, he spoke to Herr Braun and Mr. Wilkinson, who in turn, went to the coffin. A few subdued words were exchanged which I could not clearly hear, and both being apparently satisfied asked for the coffin lid to be placed in position and secured. For Herr Winkler this act was his closure, mine was yet to come.

"Mr. Harper, arrangements are in place for your father's remains to be flown to England. The German authorities have agreed that your wishes will be carried out. There are a few formalities to be undertaken, paperwork to be signed and authorised you understand, then everything will be in order." This was the first time that Mr. Wilkinson has really spoken to me. Shaking my hand firmly he turned and conferred with Herr Braun, they then shook hands as if to seal an agreement.

"I can never thank you all enough for what you have done today, I don't have the words. My mother would have been so proud of my father if she had survived to see his remains returned to the country he fought and died for. And you Herr Winkler, what can I say, How can I ever thank you? I will forever be in your debt."

"There is no need my young friend. It has been my honour to do what I felt had to be done. Your father was a very brave man, it is correct now, that he returns to England."

The coffin was carefully lifted up and carried to one of the other waiting cars. Ernst was still there, patiently waiting. There were tears in his eyes. I shook hands again with Mr. Wilkinson, Herr Braun and the other two men, thanking them for all that they had done on my behalf. Herr Winkler and I got into Ernst's car and following the other cars drove slowly out of the forest and back onto the main road. My father was on the final leg of his journey back to England, his wife, and home.

On the way back to the hotel, the other cars separated from us and went onto Munich airport. Herr Winkler explained to me that the coffin was already expected and would be given special clearance to leave for England on the next British Airways flight. My father had flown his Lancaster to Germany in 1941, and here he was now, flying back to England. I silently wondered if his crew's souls would somehow travel back with him. Inside of me I prayed that they would, re-united again, flying together for the last time.

I went inside the hotel with Herr Winkler who waited downstairs while I went up to my room and packed ready for my return to England, taking extra care to pack the briefcase and its documents he had entrusted me with.

Back in the lobby I walked over to where Herr Winkler was waiting for me. "Herr Winkler, again thank you for all you have done. Without you, none of this could have happened."

"For me Herr Harper, it is all over now, but for you it is just the beginning I think. I did what I did because I met a brave young man many years ago. This was my way of paying him and the Allies a debt of gratitude for releasing us Germans from the grip of Nazism. Goodbye now my young friend. Ernst will drive you to the airport. Take care my young friend."

A final, firm shake of hands and he was gone, walking out of my life as quickly as he had come into it. Ernst came and picked up my suitcase and motioned towards the car. I was going home with my father.

Chapter 8

England and the Final chapter?

Upon my return to England I made all necessary funeral arrangements to lay my mother and father at rest side by side to be together again after so many years. The day of the funeral was a very solemn yet joyful occasion. Representatives of the Royal Air Force and Royal British Legion were in attendance respectfully giving my father full recognition. My father's coffin was draped in the Union Flag. A guard of honour comprising of six members of the Royal Air Force Regiment accompanied his coffin from the church, and now, as his body was gently lowered into the grave alongside his wife, these six airmen fired a last salute over his coffin.

So that was the end. I stayed for a while after everybody else had left and said a few last words to both my mother and father. My only regret was that my mother hadn't survived to be here standing along side of me, but now they were at peace together - forever.

Some days after the funeral I read every piece of evidence that was held within that battered old briefcase. Reflecting on its contents and following a few days of deep thought as to my next move I wrote to the Ministry of Defence and the Foreign Office and placed before them the facts that I had been given regarding my father's part in killing Adolf Hitler in 1941 and his subsequent execution at Dachau in 1945. It was some time before I received any replies from them and to say that they were very sceptical and disbelieving would be an understatement! I also decided at this time not to communicate with either the local or national press, but to allow the Ministry of Defence and the Foreign Office the opportunity to decide on their next move, if any.

However, with perseverance and many phone conversations to various secretaries in those Government offices I eventually managed to get an appointment with the Foreign Office and met with two gentlemen and their secretaries at their Whitehall offices, who, although they were extremely polite and patiently listened to my brief summary of the evidence, gave the impression that they either did not believe the evidence I had presented to them, or were unwilling to take the matter any further without further consulting their superiors. To have this meeting though, I felt was positive and was, I suspected, a move on their part to discover just what evidence I actually had.

Leaving their offices in Whitehall I returned to my mother's house in the Lincolnshire countryside to decide upon my next move. Very well then, in the possible absence of any further communications from the Government I would draw up a plan of action.

I resolved that somehow the truth would be told - even if the consequences to me proved to be unpleasant! If the British government were not prepared to believe me and reveal the truth to the world, what then of the German, Russian and American governments? Surely they would help. And the Royal Air Force, could they deny the existence and bravery of what one of their own bomber pilots had achieved, not only acting with distinction and bravery night after night, setting course for Occupied Europe along with many other Bomber Command aircrew, but more than that, succeeding in the assassination Adolf Hitler where many others had failed. My father had made the ultimate sacrifice with his life, should he now be denied that the whole world should know the final story of his last days on this earth? That was it then. My mind was made up. I felt as if a huge electric generator was running inside of my body to power my mind so I set to work.

My first action was to write an identical letter to the German, Russian and American Embassies in London giving all the details and copies of the documents. I decided not to send the originals to any third party lest they 'disappear'! They would remain locked up in a very secure place until such time that I needed to produce them.

Disappointingly I heard nothing for many weeks until an official looking envelope appeared through my letterbox early one sunny morning. Picking it up with some trepidation I opened it up hurriedly with shaking hands from the anticipation of what I might discover within. I unfolded the neatly typed letter and began to read its contents. It was from the Air Ministry. An invitation to attend a meeting to discuss with representatives of the Ministry of Defence, the Royal Air Force, the Bomber Command Association and Royal British Legion what I had relayed at my earlier meeting with the Foreign Office several weeks ago. Far better than I could possibly have hoped for. At last somebody was taking notice!

On the day specified in the letter I duly arrived at the Air Ministry in good time. I presented the letter at the reception desk and was given directions to the appointed meeting room on the second floor. Finding the correct room, I knocked with some trepidation on the door and was invited to enter from some unseen voice within the room. Opening the door I stepped inside not being too sure what to expect. Closing the door behind me I was offered a chair in front of a desk, behind which, two officers in uniform and two men in civilian attire were seated. Sitting down in front of them I felt very disadvantaged.

One of the officers introduced himself and his fellow companions. He and the other officer were attached to the Ministry of Defence and Air Ministry and were advisors to the Prime Minister, at last I thought, now I'm getting somewhere. One of the civilians was involved in an investigative role with the Bomber Command Association the other represented the Royal British Legion. Even better I thought, my confidence now returning.

They sat in silence listening to my every word while I presented my case to them. I explained that the Foreign Office did not appear to want to pursue the matter further for whatever reason, although I was obviously wrong with this assumption, as they had obviously decided to push the matter up to a higher level.

No questions were asked of me, in fact the four said very little at all. Their spokesman did however promise to report to the Prime Minister with their recommendation as to how to proceed, if at all, no promises were given. A handshake from each of them in turn and the meeting was closed, no doubt they would now discuss between themselves what had taken place, I left in high spirits. Surely now with the Ministry of Defence, Royal Air Force, the Bomber Command Association and the Royal British Legion apparently all on my side, the Prime Minister and British Government must take notice and act!

The Royal British Legion I discovered later had previously been contacted by Mr. Wilkinson of the War Graves Commission whom I had briefly met in Germany at my father's graveside. He too realised that my father's actions and his death at Dachau must be made available to the world, and to this end he had related the whole story to them. So with these much respected and renowned organisations on my side I felt really confident.

It was late, so I had decided to stay overnight in London. A room at the Hilton had been booked on my behalf by the Royal Air Force representative. In a much better frame of mind I had a good night's sleep. In the morning I was to travel back to my home in Lincolnshire to await what I felt sure would be more positive news. The embassies would have received the documentation by now, so I felt that I had done as much as I could - for the time being. Now to wait and discover what their reactions would be.

The weeks passed slowly by and I had received no news at all, not from the German, American or Russian Embassies, the Ministry of Defence, Royal Air Force, Bomber Command Association, or either the Royal British Legion. To say I was very disappointed would be an understatement. Had they all decided to put a blanket of silence on everything or were they simply waiting for me to make my next move - not that I had one!

Then, early one morning the telephone rang. I was being summoned to Whitehall! The kindly female voice on the end of the phone line informed me that a car would collect me the following day at nine o'clock sharp. I would not require an overnight bag, as I would be brought home the same day. She informed me that at this meeting would be representatives from the American, Russian and German

Embassies, plus two very high up officials from the Foreign Office and Ministry of Defence. The Royal Air Force was also to be represented, as was the Bomber Command Association and the Royal British Legion. Action at last! I was asked to bring all documents with me, including any copies that I had. There was no suggestion that another date would be allowed if inconvenient, so it was to be tomorrow or never. Tomorrow it would be then.

I slept fitfully that night, my mind going through all sorts of imaginary scenarios as to what tomorrow might bring. Would I be arrested as soon as I arrive on some long forgotten, obscure, National Security issue, perhaps one of the many emergency measures that came into play during the Second World War and had never been repealed. I shivered at the thought. Surely that couldn't happen in England - could it? Being unable to sleep with all of these thoughts scrambling around inside of my head I decided to rise although it was still very early.

I took a long, calming shower and ate a good breakfast - although I didn't feel particularly hungry and, taking my time to dress, I was ready in plenty of time before the car arrived. This was the worst time. The waiting. Is this how my father felt before he was taken out to be shot? What he went through I could not possibly begin to imagine. He lived in a nightmare world for so long.

A sharp knock on the door announced the arrival of my transport to London and my meeting, which I silently prayed, would this time have a positive outcome. I gathered everything that I needed especially the grubby old briefcase that Herr Winkler had passed over to me in what now seemed years ago although in fact it had only been just over nine weeks.

An immaculately attired young female driver escorted me to the car and offered to place the grubby briefcase in a secure place in the boot. I gratefully declined. I was definitely not going to let this out of my sight until I had safely returned this evening!

The drive down to Whitehall was uneventful. Whether she was told not to make conversation or not I didn't know, but when I attempted to talk to her she proved to be very evasive, answering any questions with a very polite excuse of not having any knowledge as to the reason for my journey, so eventually I resigned myself to a very quiet, long journey.

I pondered over what I had done. Did my actions stir some government office or official into believing my story after all? Who exactly was I about to meet with? There was no indication from the girl on the phone last night, and I was just too taken aback to ask! The next few hours would determine the outcome, until then I had to be patient.

Arriving at a pre-arranged time and point on the outskirts of London we were met by two police motorcyclists acting as outriders. With blue lights flashing they escorted us through the heavy traffic ensuring that we were not delayed. The police escort left us at Whitehall and the car continued through security checks without delay. Pulling up outside one of the entrances to the impressive building, the driver promptly opened my door and another young lady escorted me into a lobby where, sitting behind an imposing reception desk, I was introduced to a very smartly dressed lady who shook my hand and greeted me with a very warm smile and deftly placed a visitor's pass onto my lapel. I was surprised to see that this pass had my photograph on it. How on earth did they acquire this? Walking together across the marbled floor, she guided me towards a lift. Selecting the third floor button, the lift door slid open and we stepped inside, again, as was the drive down, conversation was not encouraged.

We arrived at the third floor and she led me to a room at the end of the long carpeted corridor. On each wall were imposing paintings of prominent elderly politicians, their eyes peering down on me as if in judgement of what was to come. We arrived in front of a stout, carved oak door. Opening the door without knocking to announce our arrival, she ushered me in and then turned around and left the room, closing the door silently behind her.

Inside this room, seated at a long highly polished table placed in front of a window looking out over London were six men. One was wearing the uniform of a Royal Air Force high ranking officer, probably an Air Marshal, although my knowledge of rank insignia was a little rusty. The other men were all in civilian clothes.

"Please come in Mr. Harper and take a seat here if you will." It was the officer speaking. I slowly and hesitantly moved across to where he indicated and sat down facing him.

"Thank you so much for coming today. I am Air Marshal Dickinson and these gentlemen on my left are attaché's of the German, American and Russian Embassies here in London. The two gentlemen on my right are from the Ministry of Defence and the Foreign Office, both of a much higher position than those you have previously met I might add. But first, on behalf of Her Majesty's Government I would like to express my sincere apologies for the way you were treated when you first approached us. We really did not fully comprehend the full extent of your father's actions. You should never have been sent away in such a fashion. We can only apologise to you." Each of the other men nodded their heads in agreement.

I carefully placed my evidence on the richly coloured carpet beside my chair, taking care that the briefcase did not fall over and spill its contents on the floor. This was at least a very good start. The recognition of what my father had done was now being fully acknowledged, but I still wriggled uncomfortably in my seat. The 'big guns' were certainly here today I thought. But even with the sincere apology, was this a good omen or bad? I was about to find out. He introduced the gentlemen sitting along side him, and each in turn welcomed me most warmly. The Russian representative was not quite as welcoming as the others though. I immediately realised that if he had read the evidence that I had sent to his embassy then he may be rather annoyed about the disclosure and truth regarding how his countrymen had hidden from the world the facts, as they knew them at the time, of Hitler's fate.

"Mr. Harper. Before we start to inform you as to our findings, can I ask if you have brought all of the documentary evidence to support your claim as we requested including any copies?"

So they had already decided what their actions were going to be. From the briefcase I took out all of the documents and placed them in front of him on the desk. He reached across and placed them in his briefcase, checking first that they were all there.

"Thank you Mr. Harper. Can I have assurance that these are the only copies in existence, apart of course from those that you sent to the Embassies of Germany, Russia and America which we have here?" He pointed to a folder in front of him. I confirmed that these were the only other copies. I was by now beginning to worry as to why he was so concerned about this. I would soon find out.

Looking directly into my eyes he said. "Mr. Harper. I now would like you to sign the Official Secrets Act. This is a requirement of this meeting continuing."

He took from a folder on the desk, two A5 size sheets of paper together with a pen and indicated to me where I must sign them. Having no option, I duly signed both and slid them across the desk to him. Neatly folding them both in half, he placed one in his briefcase, the other he gave back to me after placing it inside of an envelope and sealing it down.

"You are now legally obliged, by law, not to divulge to any body what takes place this morning in this office. Failure to do so will result in immediate arrest and possible imprisonment for you. Is that quite clear Mr. Harper?" His tone of voice was now completely different to earlier, much harsher and unwelcoming. I nodded in full understanding. I had a feeling in the pit of my stomach that this meeting was not going to turn out the way I was hoping.

"We haven't contacted you before now, because your story, and these documents, required a great deal of discussion and investigation before we could come to the conclusion that we all have conclusively arrived at. I can say our decision was not reached at all lightly. But, however, it is with the full agreement of the governments involved in this matter, the German, American and Russian, that your father's extraordinary action should never be disclosed to any other person, and will never reach the domain of the general public of any nation." I looked in shock and dismay across the table at the six faces opposite me. They showed no emotion. Each face was in turn looking at me for my reaction. I was in a state of total disbelief. How could they possibly have arrived at this decision?

"We really are extremely sorry about this. We all realise what this matter means to you. But, Mr. Harper, we have to look beyond your hopes and aspirations. We have to look at what the consequences of releasing this quite remarkable story would have, not only for the nations involved, but on the whole world. We cannot accept the risk of throwing the world into political breakdown and distrust. We are in an era where the Cold War is over; Nations who once threatened other Nations with war are now almost a thing of the past. After many weeks discussing this matter, and I can assure you, at the very highest level, we are all agreed that to release this would result in one misunderstood word or misinterpreted act turning back the political clock and seriously risk plunging the world into another global conflict. Nazism in Germany could rise again and Communism could be revived. We are not prepared to risk that. This is, as I have already stated, a unanimous decision, reached by us all. There is no appeal."

I was already expecting something like this. After all, why insist that I must sign the Official Secrets Act before the Air Marshal informed me of their decision! And they wanted all copies of the evidence safely in their own hands.

"However. It is also agreed unanimously that your father should be honoured for what he did. He will be awarded a posthumous Victoria Cross. That is the very least our Government can give, to whom we all agree, was an extraordinary brave young man."

They were to be his final words. At no time did any of the other representatives present utter a single word to me. Pressing a buzzer on his desk, the door behind me opened and my escort stood there waiting to take me back to the car. The six men stood up in unison and, to their credit each came over to me and shook my hand in turn, the Air Marshal was the last. With that they exited the room through another door and they were gone, their task completed.

So that was the end, it was over.

Epilogue

More than a week had passed since the meeting at Whitehall. I had just learned from Ernst of the sad deaths of Herr Winkler, the man who had done so much for my family, and Herr Sachs. So now there was no living memory as to those terrible days of so long ago, the last links had gone. Goodbye my old friend, I owe you so much.

I often return to my mother's and father's grave. On this particular day, a bright sunny autumn morning, it seemed a million miles away from the horrors that happened at Dachau. At long last my father was buried alongside my mother, his beloved wife. He flew from England in 1941 to help defeat an enemy that threatened the whole Free World. And now, in 1989, he was back on English soil, and his beloved Lincolnshire countryside.

Will his story ever be told? I hope so at some time in the future. After all, doesn't the Official Secrets Act only apply for the lifetime of the individual who signed it? So perhaps one day when I too, lie alongside of my parents, some soul will read the documents that Herr Winkler discovered. You see, I have a confession to make. I told a little lie!

Fearing the worst and that this story would never be made public I kept the original documents. Those that I handed over were very good copies, or fakes if you like! There is a grubby old briefcase deposited along with my last will and testament with my solicitor, and it contains those original records.

In my will I have directed that these be made public, after all the Second World War will be out of all human memory with no living survivors of those days. So perhaps one day, after I have joined my parents - who knows?

THE END

Sources and acknowledgments

I have always found photographic copyright laws a proverbial 'minefield'. The photographs within this book are at least 80 plus years old and are now freely available within the public domain via the Internet, and are, I believe, free of any copyright. If I should have innocently infringed any copyright holder I now apologise.

Whilst I have made every effort over many years to locate any possible copyright holders for the photographs used it has proved to be an impossible task. My requests have either been ignored or 'bounced back' to me as being non-existent contacts, for that reason I have decided not to use many of the photographs I have obtained over many years.

As an acknowledgement some of the photographs of the 'Eagles Nest' are from 'Homes and Garden' magazine from November 1938. I have contacted the present publishers of this magazine asking for permission to use but from their response it would appear that they do not hold the copyright, as they have no evidence or documentation that they are the copyright holders. Without an original copy of that issue I cannot pursue the matter any further to give an acknowledgement to the original source. I suspect that many were taken by a certain Heinrich Hoffmann who took many thousands of photographs of Adolf Hitler pre

World War II.

The selection of photographs on the following pages illustrates the interior and exterior of Hitler's Eagle's Nest as it was pre Second World War.

Adolf Hitler's 'Eagles Nest' in the Bavarian Alps

Originally known as Haus Wachenfeld the chalet became known more commonly as the Berghof or Eagle's Nest. Ignatius Phayre, a believed pseudonym for a William George Fitzgerald, as featured in the November 1938 issue of Homes and Garden magazine, wrote the article for that magazine.

He describes the original structure as being nothing more than a hunter's shack where Hitler's widowed sister, Frau Angela Raubal, tended the building on behalf of Hitler. Hitler however, was seeking a grand mountain retreat and so a massive rebuilding programme began with Hitler being the architect behind the scheme, it was built to his specifications. Hitler used the income from his book 'Mein Kampf' – 'My Struggle', to pay the vast cost of the rebuilding.

Entering the chalet through the entrance hall the visitor would be surprised to find many cactus plants in very ornate majolica pots. Moving on into Hitler's study they would discover a modern office with a telephone exchange leading off of it making it easily possible for Hitler to make contact with his Ministers and others.

Ignatius Phayre goes on to describe in his article the interior of the chalet. The colour scheme throughout is described as a light jade green; the curtains are printed linen or damask in soft shades. Moving into library most of the books are about history, painting, music and architecture. Throughout the chalet richly coloured tapestries hang from many of the wood paneled walls and paintings and antiques are everywhere.

Author's note. Unfortunately this is all the information (at the time of going to press) that I can accurately discover. The reader should examine the following photographs for a better perspective on the chalet's interior.

A pre-Second World War postcard captioned 'Haus Wachenfeld 1935' of Hitler's retreat taken after a massive rebuilding programme to his specifications. Author's collection

The terrace overlooking the Bavarian Alps. One of Hitler's favourite views. Acknowledgement to 1938 'Home & Garden' magazine

Adolf Hitler (back towards the camera), Field Marshall Herman Goring on the left and Field Marshall von Blomberg in the centre. The chalet is visible at the top. To the lower left at the bottom of the grass slope is the grass airstrip. Acknowledgement to 1938 'Home & Garden' magazine

The external arched passageway leading onto the terrace. Hitler can be seen sitting on the second recliner. The door at the end is one of many leading into the interior. Possibly from the 1938 'Home & Garden' magazine.

Adolf Hitler's study. It was in this room that he met with British Prime Minister Neville Chamberlain. Original source unknown. Author's collection.

The sun parlour overlooking the terrace where meetings were held when weather conditions prevented meetings from being held outside on the terrace. Acknowledgement to 1938 'Home & Garden' magazine

The dining room. Hitler would have sat at the head of the table. Original source unknown. Author's collection.

*Looking out over the Bavarian Alps.
Original source unknown. Author's collection.*

The chalet had numerous tapestries hanging from the walls. The following photograph is of the same room but from a different angle. Original source unknown. Author's collection.

This photograph is of the same room as the preceding photograph and clearly displays how ornate and richly furnished the chalet's rooms were. Original source unknown. Author's collection.

A post war photograph showing bomb damage to the chalet. Avro Lancaster bombers' of RAF Bomber Command extensively bombed the Eagle's Nest. Original source unknown. Author's collection.

Hitler Imitator Reported Ready to Die in His Place

By The Associated Press.

STOCKHOLM, Sweden, April 26—The Free German Press

Headline from April 26 1945. A newspaper report of a Hitler double. Original source unknown. Author's collection.

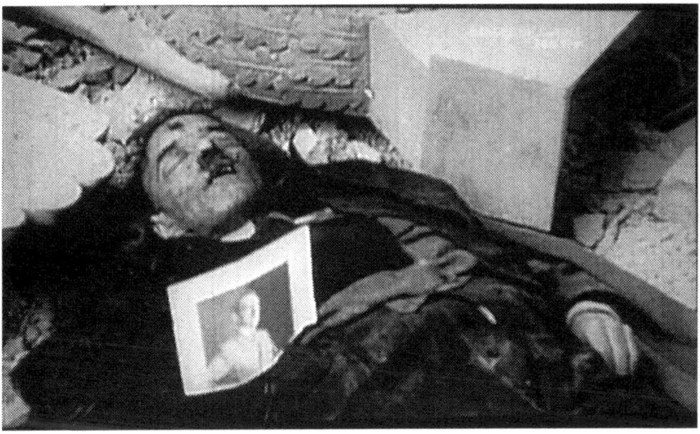

Could this corpse be a 'double' of Adolf Hitler to ensure Hitler's escape to South America? Original source unknown. Author's collection.

Printed in Great Britain
by Amazon

20869558R00127